FOREST
CANYON

D. Grant Everitt

FOREST CANYON

Enid, the pilot star of my lone life,
Enid, my early and my only love,
Enid, the loss of whom hath turned me wild—
What chance is this?
How is it I see you here?
—Alfred Tennyson, *Idylls of the King*

D. Grant Everitt

Forest Canyon

Published by EMT Communications, LLC.
Colorado Springs, CO
emtcom@comcast.net

ISBN: 979-8-9913245-3-3

Cover and Interior Design: Beryl Glass

First printing—May 2025

Contents

Acknowledgments 7

Preface 9

Introduction 11

Prologue 13

PART ONE: New Beginnings

1. Beginnings in America 19
2. History Lesson. 23
3. A Home in Enid 29
4. A Town in the Making 33
5. You're Hired 37
6. Righteous Anger 41
7. Robert Alexander (R. A.) Long's Legacy 45
8. Budding Bud. 51
9. Neighbors in Need 53
10. Fifth Street Standoff. 57
11. Boys Will Be Boys 61
12. Railroad Menagerie .69
13. Casting Stones 79
14. Mile High Hiatus 83

PART TWO: Forest Canyon

15. On the Move 91
16. Papa. 95
17. Close Call 99
18. Hidden Secrets. 103
19. Forest Canyon 107
20. No One Goes There 109

21. The Accident. 113

22. Awinita. 117

23. On the Run. 123

24. Oginalii. 127

25. Native Genius 135

26. Born to Be Free 139

27. A New Way to Pray 143

28. It's about Time. 147

29. The Utes and Climbing Bear 151

30. Deer Clan. 155

31. A Good Day to Dance. 159

32. Work and Re-Creation 163

33. Going to Water (Ama) 167

34. A Secret Way Out 171

35. Winter in the Wild. 175

36. Wolves 181

37. Back to the Garden 187

38. Sweet Sorrow 189

39. Journal's End 193

40. Now What? 197

41. Good, Bad, or Ugly 199

42. What about God? 207

PART THREE: Full Circle

43. Professor's Farewell. 215

44. Reunion 223

45. Return to Forest Canyon 227

About the Author 233

Acknowledgments

Much and many thanks to all who walked alongside me in the writing of this book, especially my wife Ann, who tolerated my physical, mental, and emotional absence at numerous points along the way.

Thanks are also due to my mentor/editor, Mike Hamel, without whom I would have written something substantially inferior, if I had written anything at all.

To Mike Haddorff, who has always encouraged me to tell more stories and introduced me to Mike Hamel.

Thanks to the early bird readers of early drafts, Ann Everitt, Stan and Sara Everitt, Claudia Gillum, Brian Trout, Tom French, and James Fightmaster, who provided valuable insight to prove improvements were necessary.

Thanks to the United Keetoowah Band of Cherokee Indians, who, through their writings, correspondence, lectures, artifacts, and personal conversations, informed and inspired me to reflect as accurately as possible the history, character, and culture of these kind and resilient people.

Also, I gratefully acknowledge those who provided much of the historical material that acquainted me with my ancestry in such vivid detail—my father, Robert Everitt, my uncle Bud Everitt, who dug especially deep and wide in his decades of research, my great uncle Bob, and lifetime friend of my parents, Jack Bowers, who insisted he knew more about our family than anyone as he and his son, John, toured me and my daughter Allison through the streets of Enid to demonstrate his acumen. What a delight!

Finally, I humbly but gladly acknowledge the Lord Jesus Christ who has graciously granted me such a fine life to reflect upon and write about, hoping that my three wonderful children, their spouses and ten delightful kids, plus future descendants, might find in these pages something of the true, good, and beautiful that they have inherited from their forefathers and foremothers.

Preface

It is said that if you seek to learn the history of your family's ancestry, you may uncover inspiring characters and admirable deeds that make you proud to be associated by blood or adoption with those from whom you are descended. You may also discover people and events in your lineage that have never been spoken of, either because they are an embarrassment or because you are the first to bring what has been hidden in the shadows into the light.

As for the nature of this story, it is neither history nor biography, though a good dose of both can be found here. Nor would it be fair to suggest that it is a work born chiefly of fiction or imagination, though both are woven in to tell the story as it should be told. As has been said of other books, "This tale is based on fact, shaped by fiction," to bring the reader some degree of enjoyment from having spent the time to read it. May it show itself to be a good story, one that follows you for years like a good friend, even after you have finally set it down. That would be my delight!

You'll likely be intrigued by the extraordinary people and occurrences spanning the last five generations of my family's lineage that you will become acquainted with in what follows. But it is the hidden history I stumbled upon as a young man that makes this story so fascinating. Secrets stashed away from the eyes of my family for decades, even after I discovered them. I will let you be the judge of whether or not such hoarding was warranted.

Introduction

When I set out several years ago to patch together a family history against the backdrop of the times in which each generation of my ancestors lived, I found myself both inspired and stunned by what I discovered. Because of the diligent research exercised by my father and his brother, I have been able to learn of my ancestry in some detail as far back as the mid-1800s when our family immigrated to America, fleeing the Great Famine of Ireland and the British Isles in hopes of shaping a better life for themselves and their progeny.

Unbeknownst to my great-great-grandparents, they were destined to be captured by the major societal changes our country was undergoing. The influx of White European immigrants had forced Native American tribes out of their homelands in the eastern portion of the United States to survive or die trying in the undeveloped and largely uninhabited territory west of the Mississippi River.

The confluence of the American Civil War, the displacement of American natives from the southwestern United States, and the Cherokee Strip Land Run in what was then Indian Territory, later to become the state of Oklahoma, created a unique subculture that swept up five generations of my family in the newly established town of Enid, Oklahoma. Major innovations in technology and transportation, the discovery and exploitation of oil, a surge in job opportunities, and rapid economic growth are just some of the major forces that provide the backdrop to this story.

After many years of research and reflection, I find myself compelled to put in print what I believe is a remarkable story that tells a tale of men, women, and their children who overcame daunting obstacles that allowed them to hand down to each subsequent generation a legacy both honorable and captivating. Although it is the story of a single family, in many ways, it contains in bold relief the struggles and triumphs all humans share, as well as the civility and moral rectitude I believe most every human heart seeks to exhibit.

Prologue

"Look out, Travis, we're goin' over! Jump!"

The muddy streets of Enid were virtually impassable by a horse-drawn wagon with a heavy load. Nevertheless, Travis's father was determined to deliver his payload of grain. The horses did their best, but the muck was too thick for the thin wheels. When both left wheels sank to their hubs, the wagon toppled, the burlap bags split, and grain was strewn across the soppy street.

"Go find Budger, son. We'll need his help gettin' out of this mess."

Travis found Budger at the Long-Bell Lumber Yard pulling twenty-foot two-by-sixes onto a flatbed. When told of the predicament, he went with Travis and quickly found a place alongside Travis's father and two other young men pushing on the tilted side of the mired wagon. The horses had been unhitched, and the freight loss lessened the wagon's burden.

Budger took charge. "Okay, ready? One, two, three, heave! Again, one, two, three, heave!" The wheels were freed, and the wagon was pushed onto solid footing. The onlookers cheered and applauded.

"Thank you kindly," Travis said as he shook Budger's hand. "Our family is truly grateful."

His given name was Bud, but everyone called him "Budger." He was big for a seventeen-year-old and capable of lifting and moving heavy objects that a half dozen men would struggle with. In the newly formed town of Enid, Oklahoma, Budger was already somewhat of a legend because of his size, strength, and stubbornness, often leading to fights with men over twice his age.

"He's a ruffian," people warned. "Don't get on his bad side. He'd rather hit you than argue for more than twenty seconds."

Quick as he was to fight, Budger was even quicker to forgive and forget. He seemed to be everybody's favorite friend, always smiling and courteous. He laughed a lot, especially at his own jokes. He was a hard worker and always on the lookout to be helpful. The kinder side of Budger's personality was his resolve to excel in everything he did, whether for his own interest or, more often, for the welfare of fellow homesteaders.

Life was hard all around, and young men had to grow up quickly. Budger was certain life could be otherwise and that he would someday, somehow, make it so. Not only strong, he was also common-sense intelligent, despite having only gone to school through the fourth grade. He viewed hardship as an opportunity and rarely let discouragement keep him down past lunch.

People always turned to Bud to help with the big stuff—moving furniture, loading coal or lumber onto wagons, shoveling rock and snow. He was frequently called on to lean his full 290+ pounds of young muscle into the side of a collapsing wall or a fully loaded farm wagon stuck in the mud and could single-handedly bring them upright. Nothing pleased him more than standing before a crowd after a feat of strength with hands on his hips and a big grin on his face, soaking in the applause and accolades.

"Way to go, Budger!" they would shout. The nick-name stuck and became a familiar greeting for all who counted him as their friend.

PART ONE:
New Beginnings

1

Beginnings in America

M y family, the Everitts, migrated from England after the Great Famine in Ireland of 1845–1849, during which the family's farm near Tamworth, Staffordshire, England, had suffered. It was either move on or starve. Jack and Elizabeth took advantage of the British government's offer to pay citizens to leave their country to reduce the number of residents who would otherwise die or burden the whole. Ireland's population alone shrank by an estimated 25 percent. The percentages were nearly as high throughout England, Wales, and Scotland.

The trip across the Atlantic was excruciating. Most passengers left behind what they couldn't carry aboard and bid farewell to their homes and communities. The conditions on the ship were cold and crowded, with little to eat and widespread sickness. Their desperate attempts to survive were fueled by the dim hope of a better life lodged in the back of their minds. Their sole aim was to endure the Atlantic crossing and cling, in weakened faith, to God's providence.

They did survive. After arriving at the Castle Garden immigration station on the southern tip of Manhattan Island, Jack, Elizabeth, and their three sons found a home in Coal Valley, Illinois, where Jack worked as a coal miner. The desire for a better life soon took them to Polk County, Nebraska, where Jack managed to buy two horses and a wagon with which he made a living as a "hack driver," hauling anything anyone needed moved from one place to another. This, along with shoeing and boarding the horses of pioneers stopping in this out-of-the-way town of Osceola, occupied most of his waking hours.

As Jack and Elizabeth's three sons matured, the two oldest brothers, George and Bill, found work in different parts of Polk County and settled in. The youngest brother, Bud, stayed on with his folks. He sensed his father was wearing himself out with the seven-day-a-week grind. He couldn't stand by any longer, so during one of his fourth-grade classes, Bud got up from his desk and jumped out of the second-story window of the schoolhouse, never to return to school again. Neither Jack nor Elizabeth hesitated to acknowledge that they needed Bud to work alongside his father despite the boy's young age. Bud's education would have to wait.

It was a hard life, but Jack was happy to be his own taskmaster when it came to working and providing for his family.

In April 1889, President Benjamin Harrison issued a decree offering free land for the taking in the Indian Territory (what later became part of the State of Oklahoma) for whoever could stake a claim to it first. High noon, September 16, 1893, was established by then-President Grover Cleveland to begin this most extensive land grab, known as the Cherokee Outlet Land Run. Over 100,000 people on horses, on foot, or in wagons lined up on the borders of the Cherokee Outlet to race to own one of 40,000 homesteads on the 6 million acres of what had formerly been Cherokee grazing land.

When Jack heard about the opportunity to own land, he sold one of his horses for money to start a new life. He, Elizabeth, and Bud took off in their Hickory High-side John Deere Buckboard Wagon with everything they owned piled high in the wagon under a dusty canvas tarp.

Sixteen-year-old Bud was by far the fittest of the three and so walked alongside the workhorse hitched to the wagon for the better part of the 400-mile journey to the soon-to-be-born town of Enid, Oklahoma. It was slow going, but they traveled day and night not to miss the once-in-a-lifetime chance to own real estate and make a fresh start in a new land.

"We'll build ourselves a fine house, Lizzy. Bud and I will start a business of some sort in town! Right, son?" Jack exclaimed with a grin that couldn't be wiped away for nothing or nobody. Just daydreaming about how life would be caused him to periodically break the silence of the monotonous miles with one arm extended to the sky and a loud "Yahoo!"

As they journeyed into Indian Territory, I will pick up the story of Jack and Elizabeth Everitt and their son, Bud—my great-grandfather. But first, I have to set the historical background against which the extraordinary events that transpired in my family's history can be adequately appreciated.

2

History Lesson

t the beginning of the 1830s, nearly 125,000 Native Americans lived on millions of acres in Georgia, Tennessee, Alabama, North Carolina, and Florida—land their ancestors had occupied and cultivated for generations. However, by the decade's end, very few natives had remained anywhere in the southeastern United States.

Each of the Seven-Clan Council members sat on the floor of the Council House atop Kituwah (also spelled *Keetoowah*) Mound discussing what should be done in response to the increasing intrusion of the Euro-Americans into their tribal lands.

Leotie (Prairie Flower), who was honored with the title *Ghigau* (Beloved Woman), spoke her mind to the chiefs and elders gathered in the Council House around the Sacred Fire. She shared this dream:

The whitetail, beaver, and hawk lived happily
in our forest with trees, berries, flowers, and all

living things until the day comes when a white fire approaches from the northeast. The fire is small at first, but soon grows to consume or force off the land all living things. The red-tailed hawk soars above to warn of this danger.

Leotie went on to explain: "The Great Spirit has shown me that our lands and our lives will be taken with bloodshed if we remain. Our traditions and ways of living will be carried away as dust by the wind. We must move on!"

The prospect of leaving their land and settling west, beyond the Mississippi River, was discussed with much emotion. On behalf of many others on the Council, Chief Falling Rock argued against the move. "Where are we to go?" he pleaded. "How will we survive if we have no land to plant and harvest? If we have no shelter? This is where the Great Spirit gave us to live. This is the home of Creator's Sacred Fire."

In the end, to leave was decided to be the wise choice. Leotie, Chief Falling Rock, and most of the Keetoowah Cherokee established themselves as Early Settlers in Arkansas and Eastern Oklahoma. It was not without hardship, but they escaped the massacres and loss experienced by their Cherokee kin who remained in the East.

Just as Leotie's dream foretold, a few years later, the U.S. government, working on behalf of European immigrants, would violently force the westward migration of nearly 125,000 Native Americans from the millions of acres they inhabited in Georgia, Tennessee, Alabama, North Carolina, and Florida. Perhaps the most notorious of the relocations occurred in 1838 when the U.S. Department of War, under President Martin Van Buren, forcibly pushed the Cherokees into Indian Territory, which was later (1907) incorporated into the state of Oklahoma in violation of a long-standing treaty. One out of every four of the estimated 17,000 Cherokee men, women, and children would die during the 1,200-mile, four-month trek.

Once the involuntary migration began, the devastated Indians, with no shoes and little clothing, traveled the distance on foot. They weren't allowed to stop in any town along the way, as townsfolk feared diseases and disruption. The natives named this horrific suffering *Nu-na-da-ul-tsun-yi*, or "the place where they cried." This tragedy is what we now speak of as the "Trail of Tears."

No longer free to remain a sovereign people in their native country, the Indians were forced to assimilate into the invading European culture or reestablish their traditional tribal way of life in the virtually unpopulated regions to the west that the U.S. government had set aside for them. They were promised by treaty that they would be free to retain their cultural and governmental autonomy with the blessing and financial support of the federal government. It soon became evident that this was anything but a fair proposition. Land quality was inferior, and the promise of self-government was never granted. These tragic migrations occurred roughly between 1831 and 1840.

By the time the Civil War started in 1861, most of the Native American Tribes east of the Mississippi River had been displaced from their homelands by the U.S. government's Indian Removal Act, initiated by President Andrew Jackson. The immigrating Europeans yearned to make their fortunes by growing cotton on these eastern lands, then occupied by indigenous people who had been there for centuries. The intruders often resorted to violent means to grab the land and push the natives farther west. They stole livestock, burned and looted houses and towns, committed mass murder, and squatted on property that did not belong to them.

The various tribes were required to reestablish themselves in the virtually uninhabitable and undeveloped territories of the Great Plains west of the Mississippi River.

Even in Eastern Oklahoma's Indian territory, there were occasional skirmishes between the Keetoowah and the increasing number of pioneers passing through or "squatting" to eke out a living on land they deemed was their right to possess. But for the most part, the Indians lived their traditions for more than thirty-five years free from disruption on the wind-swept grass-lands of the western plains. All this would change with the Cherokee Outlet Land Run in 1893, which occasioned the sudden mass influx of an estimated 100,000 opportunists looking to fashion a new life as they formed small communities in the soon-to-be State of Oklahoma.

Seemingly overnight, the Indians found themselves living alongside a collection of Europeans migrating from their homelands, displaced landowners and their slaves looking to rebound after the South's defeat in the Civil War, and carpetbaggers from the Northeast, hoping to find riches in the boom towns being built from scratch. The ensuing decades would tell whether this hodgepodge of cultures would become a melting pot of divergent peoples or an American failure.

3

A Home
in Enid

Against this historical backdrop, my great-great-grandparents and their son, Bud, found their way into Oklahoma during the Cherokee Outlet Land Run of 1893.

Because Jack owned a livery stable, horses, and a wagon, he was accustomed to hauling freight for a living between towns in Nebraska near where he lived to Oklahoma City by way of the Chisholm Trail. It passed through the sixty-mile-wide Cherokee Outlet, erroneously known as the Cherokee Strip. Consequently, Jack and Bud became quite familiar with the northeastern part of the Oklahoma Territory. There is a family story of Jack and Bud spending one night in a camp with Jesse James and his gang. One wonders what stories were shared between them. When the Land Run came, Jack knew exactly what lot he wanted for his new home and where he could stake an additional claim in downtown Enid for his livery stable and hauling business. He also knew it was twenty-some miles shorter from Hennessey on the south border of the Outlet to Enid than from the town of Caldwell, Kansas, situated north of where most would start their race.

Jack chose the Enid land office to stake his claim as it offered a natural topography and water supply superior to the other three land offices targeted by the U.S. government for claims to be filed. A train station had already designated the town of Skeleton (later renamed "Enid") as a government registry office for those participating in the Run.

A few days before the start of the Run, Jack packed up his family and belongings and made his way to the south border to ready himself for the competition to secure the best lots on offer. Being a clever man, on the day of the Run, he unhitched his horse from the wagon, kissed his wife, and bid his son farewell, then set out on his horse, Billy Bryce. He would outride those on foot or those with family and belongings in tow to secure his once-in-a-lifetime shot at a better life.

"Wish me luck!" Jack yelled over his shoulder as Lizzy and Bud stood waving farewell to the man they loved and admired.

Whether by luck, smarts, dogged determination, or divine providence, Jack's efforts were successful. With government papers in hand for the two pieces of real estate, he rode back to fetch his eagerly waiting family.

"Yahoo, yahoo, it's done! We have a new home!" Jack screamed, waving his two land deeds as he galloped toward his grinning wife and seventeen-year-old son.

The house they built was situated on a fifty-foot-wide lot and dug into the side of a hill to which they added sod blocks to make a front wall and doorway. The first of the Everitt clan to arrive in the United States now owned property they could legally call their home. Here, they lived until they could afford a less crude structure. The natural springs at what later became Government Springs Park provided water for the home, while Boggy Creek supplied water for Jack's livery stable downtown on Second and Randolph.

"I believe we're going to like living in Enid, Jack," Lizzy said.

"I think so, too, Lizzy. We're off to a good start."

4

A Town in the Making

ike all boom towns, Enid's population and economy snowballed, accompanied by inevitable growing pains. Very few citizens knew one another before arriving in those early years. Still, all held in common the opportunity for a fresh start and worked together to fashion a new town. Strangers quickly became good neighbors; they were decent folks dreaming of a better life.

Predictably, some who rushed into this town-in-the-making seized the opportunity to "serve" the new population with bootleg whiskey, gambling, and prostitution, catering primarily to the male majority. Regardless of their intentions, all who came to Enid brought their distinct traditions, ethnicities, and prejudices. These biases showed themselves in subtle and not-so-subtle ways. Negroes escaping from a culture which had enslaved their families for generations formed enclaves in unofficially designated parts of town. Slave owners from the Deep South, including not only European Whites, but also Indians, and even some wealthy Negroes, betrayed by the outcome of the Civil War, came to Enid harboring contempt, if not outright hatred, for people they considered of lesser value—especially "niggers."

The KKK was already implanted in the town's womb and would come to life in the early 1920s. Its boast was, "We have come to rid the country of foreigners, Catholics, bootleggers, and Blacks—anyone who might threaten White Americans' livelihood." Fortunately, these extreme sentiments were not widely held or expressed in public, at least early on.

Of course, the well-established presence of Indians in Oklahoma Territory was a social factor that newcomers were also required to contend with. The Dawes Act of 1887—six years before the Land Run—authorized the government to break up tribal lands into small allotments to be parceled out to any Indians registered on tribal rolls. Although the intent was to assimilate Indians into the emerging American culture, the results were disastrous.

As predicted by many Cherokees, especially the more traditional Keetoowah, much of the land formerly held communally was lost as individuals sold their plots to non-natives, eroding the traditional Indian culture. Other Indians went broke trying to farm their tiny land allotments and eventually sold out for little or nothing. Gambling and alcohol often consumed what little gains were realized by the "lucky" few who didn't sell for a loss.

The ironic tragedy was that, in due course, this land became extremely valuable as oil was discovered and commoditized by various oil concerns eager to satiate the seemingly unquenchable thirst for the "black gold." The inverse irony is that subsequent generations of Cherokee and other indigenous tribes were financially advantaged by future discoveries of oil and methane gas on many reservations still controlled to this day by the descendants of their historical tribes, including many in Oklahoma.

Through the years, the citizenry of Enid witnessed ongoing feuds between the various bands of Cherokee. Some sought to conserve their heritage and traditions by forming separate governing councils, most notably the United Keetoowah Band, who considered themselves the "Real People" and guardians of the old ways brought to Indian Territory in 1828. A distinction was often made between the traditionalist Full Bloods and the Mixed Bloods, who were more amenable to the ways of European White culture.

Many died during the power struggles to secure the right to govern the Cherokee Nation. Would the federal government allot land to the Indians in exchange for capitulating to the authorities desiring to make Oklahoma a new state in the expanding Union? Or would the government continue to honor earlier treaties that granted the Indians self-rule? This was the critical issue.

In Enid, as in most emerging communities during this era, newcomers wanting to understand and treat the various Indian tribes as a unified race found this problematic. Most Cherokees seemed to embrace their inevitable absorption into the White culture brought from the Eastern United States. Many took paying jobs in the new communities. Friends were made. Money was made. Cherokees intermarried with other tribes, with the Whites and the Negroes, and bore children of mixed blood.

However, there were also Indians, such as those of the Keetoowah Nighthawk Society, who retained the traditions and customs of their ancestors, including the secretive and sacred Stop Dance, Sacred Fire Ceremonies, Pipe Smoking, and Wampum Belts. They isolated themselves as much as possible from what they considered polluting elements destined to corrupt and harm their people.

After the Land Rush, times were tough and confusing, but the prospects of building a good life and a new community left little time to focus on the complexities of people's backgrounds, ethnicities, or traditions. A town was in the making!

5

You're Hired

Bud wiped the sweat from his brow and stretched his back. He looked across the flatbed his father had just bought and said, "Dad, I don't know how we're ever going to get this livery stable built so long as we keep getting requests to haul stuff."

"Son, hauling stuff is the only way we can survive right now," Jack replied.

They often worked together on deliveries for the lumber yard next to their lot in downtown Enid. Fortunately, Jack had chosen this particular lot for their livery stable and hauling business. It was adjacent to the Long-Bell Lumber Yard that had opened in the 300 block of East Main Street. The Long-Bell Corporation quickly grew into the country's largest and most successful chain of lumber yards. It had acquired a commercial lot in Enid to supply the material needed for this built-from-scratch town.

Jack expected a good share of his hauling business to come from his neighbor's enterprise. In the back of his mind, he also thought the location would give him good exposure to folks needing a place to shoe, board, or rent horses. Despite his hunches proving better than expected, Jack barely scraped by.

Mr. Robert Alexander (R. A.) Long, the founder of the Long-Bell Lumber Company, passed through Enid one day to check on his business when he saw Bud next door and introduced himself.

"Every time I come through town, I notice you working long hours with your father," Mr. Long said. "You appear stronger than an ox and never seem to tire, and you're always whistling or singing as you work. I sure could use someone like you in my lumber yard."

That caught Bud's attention.

"I'll pay you a good wage if your dad would be willing to give you up," R. A. added.

Bud liked the sound of that. He removed his glove and extended his huge right hand. "Mr. Long, I would be honored to work for someone like you."

"What's your name, son?" R. A. asked as they shook hands.

"Bud Everitt, sir. But most call me Budge or Budger."

"Talk to your father and tell me what you two decide."

"I'll speak with my dad, but he'll be all for it. Besides, I'm seventeen and capable of deciding what I want my future to look like. If you're around tomorrow, I'll give you my answer. If you're gone, I'll tell you right now the answer is 'yes.' When would you like me to start?"

"Well, Bud, if your father is agreeable, why don't you give him the rest of the week at your job here? You can report to Red, my yard manager, first thing Monday morning."

"How about Saturday morning?" Bud offered.

R. A. laughed. "I like your spirit, son. Saturday or Monday, you've got the job. Work it out with your current employer," he added with a wink. "Glad to have you aboard."

R. A. walked away with a smile on his face and a good feeling in his heart. *That kid has the most enormous hands and forearms I've ever seen. He's a keeper!*

Mr. Long had no way of knowing that the night before, Jack and Bud had agreed that the hauling business wasn't enough to support their family. They decided Bud should look for other work to bring in more income.

Jack was amazed when Bud told him of being hired at Long-Bell Lumber, the largest business in town.

Lizzy was delighted. "Maybe now I can fix my working men more than beans and potatoes for supper," she announced.

6

Righteous Anger

Bud reported to the lumber yard the following Monday and worked out details with Red, whereby Bud would work Monday through Friday at the yard and Saturdays with his dad at the livery stable.

"Mr. Long insisted you help your Pa one day a week," Red told Bud. "Said he couldn't afford to see the best freight and coal hauling outfit in town go under. Pay's the same—five days or six. Best spend Saturdays helping your Pa. As for Sundays, I suspect you'll be attending the new church with your Ma and Pa."

Bud made friends with everyone in the yard as the months went by. He enjoyed telling corny jokes when loading or unloading cargo for folks doing business with Long-Bell.

"That's the stupidest joke I've ever heard, Bud," cracked one customer. "Got any more like that?" Smiles and laughs all around.

Red liked having Bud working with him. He told Mr. Long that Bud had a strong work ethic and was always ready to lend a hand to ensure that orders were filled and delivered on time.

One spring day, Red heard a commotion in the alley. He ran out to see Budge pounding a man he guessed to be in his early twenties. A young Indian girl lay curled up nearby, crying, shivering, and frightened. When Red appeared, the man pulled away from Budge's grip and fled.

Red was livid. "What the hell you doing, Budge? You can't be fighting like this! We're going to see Mr. Long right now!"

R. A. looked up from his desk when Red knocked. "Come on in. The door is open."

"Hi, Red, Bud. Take a seat. So, men, what can I help you with?"

"Mr. Long," Red began. "I caught Budge fighting with some guy in the alley. He was pounding him pretty good, and I was afraid Budge was going to kill him. I know you don't like fighting, especially on the job, so I brought him to you."

R. A. looked at Bud, "This true, son? You've been fighting when you should be working?"

"I heard someone crying out back," Bud answered. "When I went to check on it, I saw a man throwing this girl down and trying to ride her. I pulled the guy off her and let him have it. It wasn't right what he was doing. The girl was crying and screaming and trying to get loose from him.

"I know we're not to be fighting at the yard, Mr. Long," Bud continued. "If you need to fire me, so be it. I'm not apologizing for what I did, and I'll do it again if need be."

"Where is this girl now?" Mr. Long asked Red.

"Don't know, sir. I came right here with Budge to see you. She's probably run off by now."

"Why don't you go check?" Mr. Long motioned to the office door with his hand. "If you find her, see if she'll return with you. If not, just come back yourself. I need to talk with Bud for a minute."

Mr. Long stood up and walked around his desk to sit beside Bud. Looking him in the eyes, R. A. calmly said, "Red did right, bringing you to see me. There's been too much anger turned to fighting in this town, and I'll have none of it in our lumber yard. But Bud, you did the right thing to protect that girl. I won't fire you, son, but I want you to think about something. Are you listening?"

Bud nodded.

R. A. pulled his chair closer to Bud's and spoke quietly. "You're one strong man; I have no doubt you could've killed that attacker if Red hadn't shown up when he did. Here's the deal. You can't let your anger grow into rage. Otherwise, it will turn into hatred and eat you alive from the inside out. You must learn to tame the flame so it will arise to burn away evil yet destroy nothing more. Do you understand?"

Bud lowered his head. "I do, Mr. Long."

7

Robert [R. A.] Long's Legacy

A kinship between R. A. Long and Bud Everitt was forged early on. R. A. schooled Bud over the course of the mentor's life, teaching by word and example the ways of business and virtue as he had learned them as a longstanding member of the Christian Church in Kansas City.

R. A. Long was an optimist and risk-taker. Before starting his lumber business at age thirty-seven, he'd gone broke twice, trying his hand as a butcher and a journeyman hauling hay. But he never lost that "can-do" attitude and wasn't afraid of work. Eventually, he grew a single lumber yard in Kansas into the largest lumber company in the world in the early 1900s, with more than 120 yards in small communities across the western and southern United States. He also vertically integrated his business by purchasing thousands of acres of timberland to supply his yards. He bought or built scores of sawmills to convert trees into lumber. He purchased or expanded railroads to transport his products to places he would otherwise not have been able to reach.

R. A. later started a newspaper in Longview, Washington, a community he designed and developed from scratch. The Longview News went on to win a Pulitzer Prize in 1981. R. A. became one of the wealthiest men in America, yet he never lost sight of his humble beginnings or his passion for doing the right thing, even when his company faced bankruptcy during the Great Depression.

His generosity and philanthropy were evident in his extensive donations to charities and churches of various denominations in the towns where he did business. He considered it only right to provide housing for his workers in the timberlands, the sawmill communities, and boom towns where housing was in short supply. If a community needed a library, school, or grocery store, he would build it and hire locals. He once said, "Using money rightly requires more good judgment than making it."

Whatever good R. A. did through his personal and business practices, whether for his family or community, grew from his daily habit of reading the Bible and praying. He claimed that many of the more productive business ideas and practices he championed came from his inspiration in these early hours of interaction with his Lord.

One example was his enlightened conviction that the common practice of clear-cutting trees insulted the

Creator, who gifted such beauty and utility to humankind. The Long-Bell Lumber Company pioneered the conservation effort to reform the lumber industry's approach to forest management well before reforestation became popular. President Roosevelt recognized R. A.'s forward thinking and invited him to the first Federal Conference on Natural Resource Conservation in 1908.

"We shall, from this day forward, replace every tree cut by Long-Bell," R. A. enthusiastically promised at a meeting in Washington, D.C., with the President and a group of like-minded businessmen.

R. A. loved the demands on body, mind, and soul that business required. He loved the camaraderie with colleagues, employees, suppliers, and customers and the on-the-job education, which together made for success. He considered the economic challenges and opportunities as icing on the cake. What he loved most was the business's positive impact on people's lives. Nothing pleased him more than seeing thousands of people flourish because of his efforts. He viewed it as a calling.

During a gathering in Kansas City a few years before he died, R. A. spoke to a group of general managers, yard managers, corporate executives, and directors about the company he'd founded.

Gentlemen, my heart is filled with thanks for every one of you. You have been part of a dream come true, growing our company into a wonder! I'm so proud of what we have accomplished together. And I'm so thankful to God and this great country for the liberty we've been provided to grow and prosper during these extraordinary times.

Freedom allows the human spirit to imagine great things. Freedom allows what humans imagine to be achieved, like innovation, commerce, and the arts. Gentlemen, we have achieved great things! But let us not lose sight of the Bible's exhortation, "You were chosen to be free. But don't use your freedom as an excuse to do anything you want. Use it as an opportunity to serve each other in love."

Thank you for joining me in bearing this responsibility with integrity and loyalty.

R. A. stood at the head of the boardroom table, steadying himself with his hands on the back of his chair as he spoke.

"One more thing, if I may. And this is of utmost importance. We're living in tough times. Folks are suffering. They're losing their homes and jobs, and far too many are in despair. It's happening all across this great country, making it difficult for Long-Bell to endure. We may not. I will do whatever I can to keep each of you employed as long as we have the money. However, things in this country will need to change if Long-Bell is to survive.

"What can we do? We can work hard and pray hard. If you can get a better job elsewhere, take it and don't look back. Your family comes first, not Long-Bell. With God's help and our good courage, I'm confident you and I WILL survive, even if the company doesn't."

This meeting occurred in the early 1930s when the Great Depression and the Dust Bowl were in their infancy. R. A. understood the hardships already threatening Long-Bell and the country—hardships he knew would continue well beyond his lifetime.

R. A. Long died on March 15, 1934. Although his riches were extensive, his fortune was significantly depleted because he was generous and refused to make drastic employee cuts when his company was languishing.

Thanks in large part to R. A.'s tenacity and good relationships with creditors, Long-Bell survived the Great Depression. The company merged with International Paper Company in 1956 and was sold outright to IPC in 1958. Long-Bell's days as a "family and friends" operation ended when it was swallowed by a behemoth with the deep pockets needed to survive.

The Everitt clan would also survive and thrive thanks to R. A.'s wisdom, generosity, and love for employees that he treated as part of his family.

8

Budding Bud

Only having a partial fourth-grade education didn't prevent Bud from being promoted through the years from Yardman to General Manager of the Enid lumber yard by 1907 at age thirty. By age thirty-seven, he was promoted to Regional Manager, overseeing more than thirty yards across Oklahoma, New Mexico, and Texas. By 1921, Bud had become a vice president of Long-Bell and the General Manager of the company's Retail Lumber Division. In time, he would administer more than 120 yards in many parts of the U. S., with R. A. offering guidance every step of the way until Mr. Long died in 1934.

As Bud matured, his reputation as a fighter vanished. He settled down and married Ruth Stanton ("Daisy") just before they turned twenty. They were well-liked by their neighbors and kept company with friends who, like themselves, were busy raising children and finding their stride in Enid's social circles. Whereas Daisy was a delight, Bud always retained a seriousness about him, garnished with an occasional joke or two. Nevertheless, he was well respected for his business acumen and strong character. When Bud was promoted to General Manager of the Enid lumber yard, R. A. told him it was time he took a name worthy of his excellent reputation and social standing.

"From now on, you should be known as 'Albert' and not Bud, Budge, or Budger."

Bud nodded to the name change, but it didn't stick. He became largely known as A. B. Everitt, but apart from business and social settings, his closest friends still called him Bud. And every so often, Budge or Budger. It was a compromise R. A. evidently accepted.

9

Neighbors
in Need

The town of Enid was born and grew up during the Second Industrial Revolution (1870–1914), when the country's population moved from a predominantly rural-agrarian lifestyle to an urban-industrial manner of living and working. This was a time of rapid scientific discovery and technological advancements in chemistry, medicine, and the mass production of consumer goods.

Natural gas, water supply, and sewage plants, available previously only in select cities, became commonplace as urbanization expanded across the United States. The enormous extension of railroads and telegraph lines after 1870 allowed unprecedented movement of people and ideas. At the same time, other new technological systems were introduced, most significantly electricity, telephones, and affordable automobiles.

Enid experienced the full benefit of this revolution. Not only were families moving from nearby ranches and farms into the young town, but people from every walk of life migrated here from around the nation for the well-paying jobs and small business start-ups that were available.

Perhaps the Second Industrial Revolution was more of a catalyst than a fundamental cause. Nevertheless, it spawned darker consequences as well. Towns like Enid wound up with shanty neighborhoods filled with drifters and tramps who were often sources of violence. Many desperately poor, unskilled, non-English-speaking workers immigrated from Europe. Emancipated yet destitute Negro and Indian slaves looking to escape the poverty and oppression they had known in the South found their way to Enid and other boom towns, only to be ostracized by the majority and exempted from economic opportunity.

Some months after A. B. was made manager of the Enid Long-Bell Lumber Yard, he brought word of this horrid reality to Mr. Long's attention in his Kansas City office.

"What do you think can be done about it, A. B.?" Mr. Long asked.

"I'm not sure," A. B. said. "Maybe Washington would have a solution now that Oklahoma is a state. Or perhaps our governor and legislators in Guthrie have some good ideas."

Mr. Long leaned across his desk, looking intently at A. B. "If your father has a horse in his stable that needs to be fed, does he send a telegraph to the President of the United States or the Governor of Oklahoma asking for food, knowing he has an ample supply of hay and oats at hand?"

"No," A. B. replied. "That makes no sense. A man should be responsible for what's his."

R. A. nodded. "So, if these folks are as desperate as you say, whose responsibility is it to care for them? They're not our horses, but they are our neighbors. They're fellow human beings made in the image of their Creator, just like you and me. Since they're in our 'stable,' so to speak, we should be the ones looking out for them. What do you think? Does Long-Bell have a part to play in this?"

A. B. and Mr. Long took only an hour or so to devise a plan.

"Okay, A. B., I like it," R. A. said. "You get to know some of these folks and offer to provide tutors to help educate their kids. Use some of your lumber-yard prof-its to pay for the tutors. Even if they volunteer, I want you to pay them. I want them to be committed."

R. A. was only getting started.

"Also, if some of your neighbors have run-down houses, I'll supply the materials from here in KC at my expense to fix them up. But you must get some of your customers to help them and teach the homeowners some skills along the way. I'll pay the contractors to supervise the jobs, and any subs needed to ensure the work is done right. You connect the right people with their needy neighbors, okay?"

A. B. wholeheartedly agreed.

"Sounds pretty exciting, doesn't it, son?" R. A. concluded. "We've both received enough treasure to keep us cheerful, and the yard in Enid has been amply blessed, wouldn't you agree? I've come to experience that there's even more joy in giving than in getting. What do you say? Let's go make some of our good neighbors in Enid happy!"

10

Fifth Street Standoff

"A. B., we've got to put a stop to this!" Greeley exclaimed early one morning.

"Agreed," A. B. emphatically replied.

Word had leaked to Greeley McKeever, a prominent businessman in Enid, that the KKK intended to disrupt a Negro spring picnic planned for Saturday at Government Springs Park. At the time, the Negro population of Enid was less than 500 people who mostly lived in the Southern Heights neighborhood alongside many Native Americans. With baskets of food and blankets in hand, they intended to parade from their homes to the park.

A. B. and Greeley went to the merchants in downtown Enid to gather resistance to the Klan but found no one interested in getting involved. Many were active Klan members or sympathized with the KKK's intentions.

"Well, A. B., what should we do?" Greeley asked.

"Doesn't matter how many of us there are," A. B. replied. "We have to do what's right."

When Saturday arrived, the two men made their way to Fifth Street, which ran north from the Southern Heights district to Government Springs Park. As the hopeful picnickers began their parade, A. B. and Greeley walked ahead, hoping and praying there would be no trouble. But as they approached the park, a large group of white-hooded Klansmen, white crosses and various weapons clearly visible, marched toward them.

"Get out of our way!" one Klansman shouted. "We have no fight with you, but we aim to put an end to this illegal nigger gathering."

As they told the story later, both men admitted being terrified, but with hands on hips, they stood their ground in the middle of Fifth Street with the Negroes at their backs and the KKK in their faces.

"You'll have to come through us first," A. B. said more confidently than he felt.

"Go back to your homes," Greeley added. "We know who you are hiding behind those hoods and robes. Jenks, Marvin, Otis, what the hell do you think you're doing? Are you looking to destroy our town with this escapade? And Jenks, I can't believe you've dragged your two boys out here to take part in this. Go home, all of you!"

Harsh and loud words were exchanged between the Klansmen and the two big men opposing them. It may have been A. B.'s and Greeley's reputation in the community, or it may have been their imposing stature, or maybe the otherwise upright citizens of Enid came to their senses. Likely, a combination of the three turned the White mob back and scattered them to their homes.

A. B. and Greeley, with sweat staining their shirts, looked at each other and sighed in relief as they walked away. The Negroes went on to enjoy their picnic in the park.

A few days after this confrontation in Enid, a similar conflict arose in Tulsa, where, over the course of eighteen hours, one of the worst incidents of racial violence in U.S. history occurred. Hundreds of people were killed, and thousands were left homeless.

Although racism was not dead in Enid, at least it had gone underground for the most part, allowing the community to move forward with some degree of civility. The overt activities of the KKK diminished rapidly in Enid and throughout the state. By 1928, the Klan's membership in Oklahoma was negligible.

A fascinating footnote should be added. A few months after the standoff on Fifth Street, A. B. was talking to one of his Negro customers at the cash register. "Seems like I'm seeing more of you folks coming in these days, Elijah

"Mr. Everitt," Elijah replied, "we've spread the word about what you and Mr. McKeever done. We said your lumber yard and Mr. McKeever's bank deserve our business, not only from Enid but from all around, from anyone who can get here. The Jews, Catholics, and Indians feel the same."

No one could have foreseen how important this would be for the survival of these two businesses in the forthcoming Great Depression. A. B. acknowledged this when he said, "Treating people honorably often has its unexpected rewards."

11

Boys Will
Be Boys

s A. B.'s reputation and status grew with the continued success of the Enid yard, his family settled
into a secure and comfortable life. His strong work
ethic was repeatedly rewarded as he strove to be the
best at all he set his mind to. Consequently, this left
little time for the family. Daisy was left to manage the
household and oversee their three boys, except when
working alongside their father in the business. At
home, Les, John, and Bob cared for the horse, the cow,
and some chickens. Les made a deal with his younger
brother, John, whereby Les would tend to the front end
of each animal by feeding it while John tended to the
back end. John always mentioned to family members
that he thought he might have been outsmarted.

There was little time left for socializing between
school, sports, chores at home, and work in the lumber yard. Although the Everitts were Enid Presbyterian
Church members, their attendance was spotty. Theirs
was more of a convenient Christianity than anything too

devout. Most everyone in their social circles attended the Presbyterian or Methodist churches in Enid. When they could carve out the time for Sunday morning services, it proved perfect for catching up with neighbors and periodically sharing meals with friends afterward. The duty of attending worship services with parents was, for the boys, a total bore. Their minds were usually elsewhere as they sat listening to sermons, songs, and prayers. Like all their friends, they were "Christians," but that mostly meant trying to be good and staying out of trouble. The whole concept of God was fuzzy.

Still, mischief wasn't beyond the boys' horizon as they grew into their teens. Les, in particular, ran with a somewhat rowdy crowd, most of whom were on the high school football team with him. Because they often failed to attend classes, the principal, Mr. Waller, would not allow a bunch of them to graduate after their senior year and held them back. Because Dewitt Waller was also the football coach, some speculated that perhaps his motives for holding the kids back were mixed.

Les had been working part-time in the Enid yard and a few smaller yards in neighboring towns since he was nine years old, starting at a dollar a day. From the beginning, his father had been his boss and thought it would be good discipline and training to get the boy working at a young age. When he graduated from high school in 1919, Les went to work full-time for Long-Bell. By this time, he had developed into a full-grown man. He was quite handsome and had an inviting personality. He had his father's physical stature, which, combined with years of football and hard labor in the lumber yard, made him rock solid and strong as an ox, as the saying goes.

When his dad was convinced he had the right stuff, Les was progressively moved into positions in the yard with more responsibilities and better pay. Still, by the time he'd given nearly ten years to the company, alongside his schooling, sports, and other activities, Les was increasingly discontent. Like many young men after high school, he wasn't sure he liked the career he saw being laid out before him. Nevertheless, he stuck it out for one more year until, in the spring of 1920, he told his father he wanted to stop working in the yard, at least for a while.

"Dad, I want to see what kind of country there is beyond Garfield County. I think it will do me good to get out of Enid for a bit and give some thought to who I really am and where I belong."

"What are you thinking?" A. B. asked, trying to hide his uneasiness. "Where would you like to go?"

"I keep hearing good things about Colorado," Les replied. "The Rocky Mountains are said to be beautiful, and a lot is going on out there." Les held his breath and tried to read his father's reaction.

A. B. kept his composure, but his face told Les he thought this was a mistake.

Next came the questions.

"You know, Colorado is quite a way from here, right? How long do you expect you'll be gone? Do you plan on coming back to Enid?"

"Sure, sure," Les said. "I mean, probably. Enid's my home. You, Mom, and all my friends are here. I just want to take a break. Instead of dreaming about what's happening out West, I want to see it myself. If things go well, I'm thinking maybe a year or so, two at the most. But I'm coming home, don't worry."

Les was unaware that Mr. Long had recently asked A. B. to move to Kansas City so they could work together more effectively.

As A. B. listened to his son's proposal, he couldn't help but think about the potential changes it would bring to their lives. However, he chose to keep these thoughts to himself and instead expressed his support for his son's decision. "You'll need to talk with your mom about it, but I think it's a grand idea. Adventure is in your blood. The Everitts have always explored new places and ways of doing things."

Although A. B. put on the best act he could, he was emotionally conflicted about what might happen to his son. Yet, he figured Les, now nineteen, was an adult, and it would be cruel to forbid him the opportunity to go, no matter how naïve he was about what awaited him in Colorado.

"I'll see about holding a job for you at the yard so

you'll have something to return to," A. B. added—anything to entice Les to return.

Daisy and A. B. invited several of Les's good friends and their parents to a sendoff party at the Everitt home the night before their son was due to leave. The adults provided plenty of hugs and handshakes, and Les's buddies gave him an overabundance of pats on the back and relentless teasing about escaping Enid without them.

The next morning, A. B. insisted that Les wear a tie and suit coat on the train. Les obliged reluctantly. There was little conversation between them during the three-hour drive to the Wichita, Kansas, train station to catch the Atchison, Topeka, Santa Fe (ATSF) train that would transport Les to Denver. Les was absorbed in thought, wondering if he was making a big mistake in leaving Enid.

"Drop us a letter or postcard now and then, won't you, son?"

"For sure," Les said, wondering if he really would take time to do it. "Dad, tell Mom I love her. Don't forget me, okay?"

At the station, A. B. popped open the rumble seat on the family's Model A and carried his son's only piece of luggage to the ticket counter and onto the platform to wait with Les for his train. A. B. had business in Kansas City at the Long-Bell headquarters after seeing Les get on the train in Wichita. Still, he was in no hurry to launch his youngest son into the unknown regions of Colorado. It felt as if he was sending him off to join a war from which he might never return.

"Do you think you have enough money?" A. B. asked. "You might need to buy more clothes if it gets cold in the mountains. You'll be careful, right?" A. B. knew he sounded like an over-protective mother, but he didn't know how else to say goodbye.

Les sensed his father was nervous about the whole experience and likely wanted to talk him out of taking the journey. But he kept these thoughts to himself. His dad's awkward behavior briefly made him consider changing his mind and retreating into the familiar life back in Enid. Instead, he pushed through the emotions of the moment, took his bag from his dad, and turned to the train just braking its way into the station. Like ants abandoning a kicked anthill, passengers scurried from each train car down the line. A. B. and Les stood on the platform among a fresh group of travelers waiting to board. In short order, the train whistle sounded. "All aboard!"

"Son, I have something I want to give you," A. B. said. "When you were born, I bought a newly minted 1901 U.S. silver dollar to commemorate your coming into the world and into your mother's and my lives. That was a special day. I kept this coin in the top drawer of my desk in the lumber yard to remind me of you when you were out of my sight. Now, I want you to take it to Colorado, not to spend, but to prompt you to remember your family in Enid and how much we love you and miss you. I don't believe in good luck charms, but please take this silver dollar, knowing that we are with you, even though separated by miles. This coin is very special to me, and so are you. May God go with you."

A. B. gave his son a firm handshake and a bear hug to seal their goodbyes.

As his father turned and walked away, Les, for the first time, sensed being truly on his own. He fought with the thought that he might never see his family and friends again. His gut went hollow.

12

Railroad Menagerie

The train ride from Wichita took two days and involved two transfers before Les was deposited in Denver. As soon as Les boarded the train, he wished he hadn't. He found his seat and settled into Seat 1, Row 14, Car 7.

"You're in my seat, move!" barked a large, hairy man standing in the middle aisle of the train car, glaring at Les. Startled, Les looked into the face from which the order came and sized him up. About the same proportions as Les, but fatter with meanness covering his face like lotion and a ballcap with the words *Chaplin Refining Co.* written above the bill of the hat. Probably a jobber on an oil rig. Unlike most on the train who dressed up for the occasion, this rough-neck, some ten years older than Les, was filthy from top to bottom, inside and out. The man's hunched, oversized shoulders and arms, accompanied by his large nostrils and extended jaw, made him look like a gorilla.

Les said to himself, *I bet I could take him if it comes to that.* The train lurched forward as it left the station.

"I said, move; you're in my seat."

Les bit his lip, pulled his train ticket from his pocket, and thrust it in the tough guy's face. "See here, Seat 1, Row 14, Car 7."

"I don't give a damn what your god-damn ticket says; my seat is where I'm going to sit next to the window. Get your sorry ass up and out of it, NOW!"

Les tried to end the loud exchange by turning his eyes to the window, but the man was relentless. By this time, everyone in Car 7 was giving attention to the quarrel, and most were on edge. A train attendant in uniform quickly made his way down the center aisle and, somewhat out of breath, inquired, "What seems to be the problem here, gentlemen?"

Without taking his stare off Les, the foul-mouthed intruder responded. "This fat kid's got my seat, and I want it."

Les was red-faced and fuming. "Fat kid, eh?" Les muttered under his breath. "Well, this 'fat kid' is ready for you anytime, anywhere. Why, I'll take this tie of mine, wrap it around your neck, drag you kickin' and screamin' to the back of the car and boot you out onto the tracks!"

"Might I see your ticket, sir?" the attendant asked Les with his hand extended. The smile and soft look in his eyes alerted Les to the steward's strategy to neutralize the situation. He was silently inviting Les to join him in the effort.

"Well, it does seem you are in the proper seat, Mr. Everitt. Seat 1, Row 14, Car 7."

"Let me see that, you stupid nigger!" The hothead ripped the ticket from the attendant's hand, read it, compared it to the label pasted on the rail above Les's seat and ripped it up. "Your name 'Everitt,' fat boy?" the bully demanded.

"Yep, what's yours?" Les asked, hoping to lower the emotional level of the conversation. But he wanted to make a soft jab and continued, "Bet it's not Everitt, is it?"

"Sir, may I look at your ticket?" the Negro steward interrupted. "Rulon Barker. Well, Mr. Barker, we happen to have an empty window seat in Car 6. I would be happy to upgrade you to it at no extra charge. The seats in Car 6 are all genuine leather and substantially wider. Can I interest you in my offer, Mr. Barker, or should I upgrade Mr. Everitt here and allow you to sit in this smaller seat?"

Barker glared with disdain one more time at Les who was smiling ever so perfectly as if to say, "Got ya, dimwit"; not so much a boast as a means to cool his primordial rage. Rulon thrust his luggage at the steward. "Okay, nigger, take me to my fancy seat."

Les leaned back and hiked his legs up onto the empty seat next to him. *Hope nobody else gets assigned this seat*, he thought.

The attendant returned and said, "I apologize for Mr. Barker's behavior. I trust we will not see him in this car again. Thank you for your cooperation and understanding."

Les sat up. "I'm glad it's over and ended well. Am I entitled to relax on both these seats for the remainder of the trip?"

"Indeed, you are." With a smile, the attendant added, "Blessed are the meek, for they shall inherit both seats, saith the Lord. Or, somethin' like that." Both men enjoyed a laugh.

I like that man, Les told himself. *Colored or not, he's a wise, kind soul. He ain't no 'nigger,' no matter Barker's empty-headed assertion.*

The word *nigger* always repulsed Les. The use of the word was strictly forbidden in the Everitt household, as was the word *Injun*.

No sooner had Les loosened his tie, leaned back, and closed his eyes than he heard a woman's voice, "Is this seat taken, young man?"

As he opened his eyes, Les saw a large, imposing figure plopping herself into the seat next to him. He pulled his legs around and placed his feet on the floor. She appeared to be about his mother's age, yet considerably larger on top and behind. It became immediately apparent that she was a talker, deluded by the notion that everyone was interested in listening to her incessantly talk about herself.

"My name's Betty," she said, grabbing Les's hand and vigorously shaking it. "My friends call me Bouncing Betty. I guess it's because my whole body bounces when I walk." Les figured he must have seemed to Betty an easy audience. After the brief courtesy of pretending to be interested, he tuned her out as she rambled on and on. He concluded he would learn as much by ignoring her as by listening to every word. Instead, he turned his attention to the blind boy in Seat 3, Row 13. He sat next to his mother, who was gazing out the window. The boy's head swung from side to side, but his posture and facial expression never changed.

How different my life would be if I couldn't see, Les thought. *What do blind people see on the other side of their eyelids? Are there images or just darkness, day and night, every day? What do the blind think about? Are their thoughts in color or black and white? When his mother describes what a car or a train looks like, or a cow she sees from the moving train, does what he imagines look like what she sees? Are blind people more content to live without the distractions of what their eyes can't see? Or are they always frustrated, wondering what they are missing? I wonder . . .*

Betty continued her monologue, answering her own questions posed to Les, from whom not a word was forthcoming. He was by now totally engrossed in his own self-absorbed contemplations. For a long time, Les thought, *I have been deprived of my own acquaintance.*

Now, in leaving Enid, will I meet myself and learn if I like myself or not?

From across the aisle, the skinny husband hollered, "Betty, for god's sake, leave that young man alone! Get yourself back over here and help me with this crossword puzzle!"

"Oh, Orvil, quit your blabbering. This young man is quite interesting."

Betty wobbled her way across the aisle and plopped into her seat with a thud.

The train clicked on.

The day's light gave way to night.

The train clicked on.

Les stretched and stood, counting the rows on his way to the toilet at the back of the car. In Row 21 sat an elderly man staring at his fingers held in his lap. He seemed lost in some kind of sadness. When he returned to his seat, Les saw the man in the same posture. Too embarrassed to approach the melancholy man and learn his story, Les took his seat, propped himself against the side of the car, and stretched his legs over Seats 1 and 2. He passed the time fabricating his own story about the old man in Row 21. The darkness of the night stimulated his imagination.

There sits Charlie, staring out the window into the void. He has lost Martha, his wife of sixty-two years. It's been almost three years since she died, but he still hasn't let go. Charlie doesn't know how. Two of his kids are scattered across the country. His favorite daughter lives abroad. She rarely sends him a letter. None have contacted him since Martha's funeral. He's not finding living alone to be easy. It's a lonely, eventless life.

Off now to California to visit his oldest son, Nathan, whom he had to beg to let him come visit. He wonders if the visit is wise. "Am I just being selfish, dropping in and interrupting Nathan's and his family's lives. I've had my turn at bat. Now it's time for me to get out of the way. It's the kids' turn. Besides, what can I really add to their lives, to anyone's life? Martha's gone. All my friends have died or are wasting away in some old folks' home. I'm just a fading photograph, still breathing. Another piece of furniture to walk around or bump into. A small, worn-down table in the corner of the living room on which to place a cold cup of coffee or the leftovers of the morning paper.

As Les envisioned Charlie's life, he was haunted by the disturbing thought that it was perhaps his own life he was questioning. *When I'm as old as Charlie, will I too be anonymous? Does anyone on this train even know this old man's real name, let alone his story? Maybe I should go sit with him and learn the truth about who he is. Likely, "Charlie" had a happy upbringing, became respected as "Chuck" in college, and as he began his career, was admired as "Charles" when he achieved success. But now, here he is, "Charlie" again, kindly admired by those who remember him, but set aside by everyone else. Will this be my legacy, too? I wonder, is this all there is to expect from life?*

Les was beginning to get depressed with his manufactured story, wondering if he could give it a happy ending. Instead, he let the story fade, knowing that once he arrived in Denver, he would disembark, and Charlie would likely travel on to California or some other unknown destination.

It was late at night, and Car 7 was quiet. Les lay on Seats 1 and 2 and threw his jacket over his head. Sleep came easily as the rhythm of the wheels clicking their way over the tracks lulled him to sleep. He suspected that his invented "Charlie" was also asleep in Row 21.

When Les wiped the sleep from his eyes the next morning, he was greeted by a young towhead and her dolly peering down on him from over the top of the seat in Row 13. "Good morning, little girl. What is your doll's name?" Her reply was a scowl with a tongue extended from her mouth, then she quickly disappeared. Les ignored the adorable wake-up call, adjusted his clothing and sleep-worn hair, and prepared for the last leg of his train ride into Denver.

His eyes were drawn to the landscape outside his window. *More of the same,* he noted. And then the towhead appeared slowly peeking over the seatback a second time. Two small eyes watched Les for a moment and then disappeared, replaced by two smaller eyes sewn on the face of a raggedy doll.

"Hi there. Where is your friend?" Les asked.

Two more eyes and the whole face of the towhead suddenly appeared next to the doll.

"I think your doll is lovely. Does she have a name?"

"Annie," came the answer. "My name is Daisy."

"Well, nice to meet the both of you. My name is Les. Guess what? My mother's name is Daisy, too."

She grimaced and shook her head in disbelief, just as from over the seat came the command, "Daisy, sit down and stop bothering the man. Here, eat your snack."

There was a whine and a whimper, but mother was to be obeyed. Then the attractive young mother turned and made herself known over the back of the seat with a smile and an apology. "Sorry about that; it's been a long trip."

"No apology needed," Les replied with a wink and a smile of his own. "You have raised your two girls very well. I saw and heard nothing from them all this way. Some would consider that a miracle. It was a delight to be greeted by two lovely young ladies this morning. My name is Les. And you are?"

"Patience," she said with a titter. "Just kidding. I'm Clare. Pleased to meet you," she said cheerfully with her hand extended.

If Les had not been so desperate to visit the toilet, he would have continued with the pleasing conversation. Instead, he wished Clare and her daughter a pleasant journey and excused himself, embarrassed by his urgency. As he hurried to the rear of the car, he thought, *I like children. Maybe when I come back home, I'll marry Madge, and we'll have some kids of our own.*

13

Casting Stones

O nce he arrived at Union Station in Denver, Les said goodbye to Clare, Daisy, and Annie. He dropped his parents a postcard informing them of his safe arrival.

> I've never seen such a place as this! The snow-capped mountains to the west, standing tall against a clear blue sky, are a sight to behold. This place is teeming with life. There is so much happening here, my head is spinning! Thanks for letting me come.
>
> Lots of love, Les

Les was off to a promising start on his grand adventure. As he glanced around the station, he caught a glimpse of "Charlie" in the embrace of a younger woman, no doubt his daughter, suffocating him with kisses while three children fondly hugged his legs and bounced around him like popcorn in a hot kettle. They were clearly delighted to greet their visiting Papa. Through his now-moist eyes, Les could see that Charlie wasn't so old or lonely after all.

Exploring the station with his belongings on his back, Les saw a display with brochures advertising free transportation to Rocky Mountain National Park with bargain rates at the famous Stanley Hotel. Having no plan of where to go once he got to Denver, Les thought the offer sounded like an excellent way to spend some of the money he'd saved for his adventurous journey.

As he sat waiting for the carriage to the Stanley, his thoughts turned back to the train ride. It occurred to him that the trip was about more than transportation from Wichita to Denver. It was the first episode in his quest to "find himself," to discover who he was from the inside out.

I think I'm kind of scared about growing up, Les surmised. *I'm not sure how I should relate to strangers, especially ones so different from me.*

It struck him that when he first boarded the train, all the people seemed like dim shadows who only gained dimension and color as he met them face-to-face. *Who was I to them?* Les wondered. *Who are they to me? Was Rulon Barker simply a bully, or had he been damaged somewhere along the way? And what about Bouncing Betty? She wasn't shy about openly naming herself, overweight and desperate to be known. Am I as honest with myself as Betty seems to be about who she is?*

As he recounted each person he connected with on the train—Rulon, Betty, Orvil, Clare, Daisy, Annie, Charlie, and the gracious attendant—like a knife to his heart, he was stunned by the thought that his fellow travelers, whom he had silently judged as lesser, were a composite of his own lesser self. He had wrongly imagined himself above them all, even those whom he found pleasant.

What an embarrassment I am to myself to discover my arrogant and selfish attitude. How might I rid myself of this foolish pride and see deeper and more graciously into the souls of others?

Les left his guilt behind in Union Station. Within an hour, he was on his way to Rocky Mountain National Park.

14

Mile High Hiatus

In a second postcard with a colored picture of the Stanley Hotel on the front, Les wrote,

Hi Mom and Dad, I'm in a mountain village called Estes Park in a valley beneath a huge mountain called Long's Peak. Wow! This place is gorgeous. Lush meadows everywhere are blanketed with wildflowers. Each time I look up, that enormous mountain stares at me. The air here is different, so clean and crisp. It's kind of like breathing cool, fresh water. It's hard to explain, but I love it!

I've been here for nearly a week, staying at this grand hotel, trying to figure out where I might go next. I've never slept better or had such great food. The hotel even has a kind of oyster they call Rocky Mountain Oysters. They're kind of chewy but delicious. Now I'm ready to explore some of the backcountry of this new place they call Rocky Mountain National Park and spend a few days hiking and camping underneath these gigantic peaks. First, I'll need to round up a few supplies. I'm so excited! This country would make your spirits fly. We all need to come here together someday.

Love, Les

With no further word from Les after the two post-cards, A. B. and Daisy's thoughts often took them to dark places.

"Now, Daisy, let's not allow our imaginations to get the best of us," A. B. said to his wife. "Les said he might be gone as much as two years. Let's choose to believe the best. He's likely having a great time. Our boy has common sense and will no doubt stay out of trouble. We can trust him and the good Lord to work it all out."

Time passed. Les and his family did not communicate for over a year. Incidents occurred that kept Les from writing, and without a mailing address for their son, the Everitts had no way to tell him about their move to Kansas City. The transfer to KC had been in the works for a while, as R. A. was grooming A. B. to supervise more than thirty of the retail lumber yards the company owned. A. B. regularly traveled between KC and Enid. He was in KC when he heard Les had returned.

"He's back, Daisy!" A. B. exclaimed. "Our boy is back! Let's drive to Enid in the morning and surprise him. Red called me from the yard and said Les came looking for me when no one was at the house. Red explained everything to him and then gave me a call. He's bunking at Red's for the night. I can't wait to see him!"

When the Everitts finally reunited, their emotions ran raw. They embraced with kisses, smiles, and a generous dose of tears all around. All three were anxious to fill each other in on the months they had been apart. They found a table at a nearby café and talked over food for the next two hours.

A. B. spoke of his promotion and the move to Kansas City. He told how Mr. Long had agreed to hold the manager's job in Enid for Les while he was gone, so long as A. B. moved to Kansas City and managed his new responsibilities. A. B. also had to ensure the Enid yard didn't miss its sales numbers. This meant frequent trips and long days in each community, but A. B. gave himself to the challenge. He believed Les would someday come home and would need the job.

As always, A. B. proved himself capable. Not only did the Enid yard continue to thrive, but the retail lumber division exceeded everyone's expectations, including R.A. Long's.

Daisy spoke of life in the big city: new friends, new sights, and a new home filled with many nice things.

"Oh, Les, you'll certainly come to visit us soon, won't you?" she asked more than once. "You look so grown up. It's wonderful to have you back!"

Although Les was weary from the long journey home, he did his best to highlight some of his experiences. "Although I missed you both and all my friends here for sure, I believe it was good that I went to Colorado. I learned so much about myself and how differently other people live. And Colorado is gorgeous. I'm sure I'll go back someday. But now I'm glad to be home."

"Your mother and I agreed to keep our home here in Enid so I would have a place to stay when I came to check on the lumber yard," A. B. told his son. "Unless you have other plans, we want you to live there and take care of the place when I'm in KC. Does that sound agreeable?"

"Sounds great, Dad. I can't wait to plop down in my own bed."

Les quickly picked up where he left off with his Enid friends and settled into the rhythm of work and recreation. He enjoyed staying at the home he grew up in and gratefully and cheerfully accepted the manager's position at the Enid yard. The employees were pleased to finally have someone to provide full-time leadership on-site. Employees, customers, old friends, and business associates saw a level of maturity and confidence in Les that he hadn't possessed before he left Enid.

Naturally, everyone was curious about Les's time away. "Did you make it to Colorado? How did you survive? Who did you meet? Where did you go? Was it ever dangerous or frightening? Did you see any wild animals? Was there a lot of snow in the mountains?"

Les willingly answered people's questions but always spoke in generalities and offered few specifics, even to his parents. "The Rocky Mountains are huge and quite beautiful," he volunteered. "And there's lots of activity. People are moving there in droves, mostly to find work, I suspect. The towns are all abuzz, especially Denver."

In conversations with one another, friends agreed that Les seemed to be keeping secrets without being overly aloof. Over time, they were satisfied with his vague summary of his time away.

One day, after Les had been on the job for several months, R. A. said to A. B. "I think your boy has become a man. Let's give him the respect he deserves, just as I did for you when you took over the Enid yard. From here on out, let Leslie Grant Everitt be known as L. G. What do you say?"

"I like it," A. B. responded with a nod. "I suspect Les will like it too once he hears it spoken about town—L. G. Everitt. It rolls easily off the tongue."

L. G. also liked the change and what it signified. Over time, he settled comfortably into Enid's social circles and the job at the lumber yard. Not too long after his return, he reconnected with one of his high school girlfriends, Madge Millard. One night, they decided to drive to the nearby town of Claremore and get married the day after Christmas. Life was good all around.

But it was about to take a hard turn.

PART TWO:
Forest Canyon

15

On the Move

I (David Everitt) moved to Colorado when I was three. My grandfather had purchased the Gould Lumber Company in Fort Collins. Mrs. Gould was selling because her husband had recently died, and she had no use for an old lumber yard. She felt she would be better off with the money from the sale.

"Well, son," my grandfather, Les, known as L. G., said to my father, Bob, "What do you think? Shall we go and take a look? It would mean you'd have to live in Colorado and manage this yard."

This wasn't my dad's first encounter with Fort Collins. He had driven through the city on his honeymoon in 1948, and both he and my mom thought it was a lovely town.

"It's worth a trip to check it out," my dad agreed. "Who knows, right?"

L. G. negotiated a deal with Mrs. Gould and her attorney over the phone. Then, he and Dad made the day's drive from Enid to Fort Collins, talking through all the "what ifs" on the way. When they arrived, they found the lumber yard in terrible disrepair, likely due to Mr. Gould's failing health before his death. The underlying structure was sound; it had "good bones," as they say, but restoring the place to working order would take a considerable sum. They agreed it was a gamble, but they liked the look and feel of the community.

"Okay, Bob," L. G. said. "If you're willing to bring your young family here, let's do it."

When they told Mrs. Gould they were ready to sign the deal, she balked. "I need $5,000 more, or I'm not selling."

Despite their sense of being mistreated, they agreed to the revised price. L. G. paid $35,000 for the real estate, inventory, and equipment. The new owners would be the Currell Lumber Company. L. G. owned 50 percent, and his partner, R. T. Currell, owned the other half. L. G. and Mr. Currell had been buying up small yards in Oklahoma while they continued working for Long-Bell Lumber.

Eventually, my dad bought Grandad's and Mr. Currell's stock in the Fort Collins yard and changed the name to Everitt Lumber Company. It would be the first of many Everitt Lumber Yards purchased by Dad and Grandad in the following years.

Mom and Dad were excited about this new chapter in their lives as they moved from Enid, Oklahoma, to Fort Collins, Colorado, in 1953. I was as excited as a three-year-old could be. Our first home was the El Palomino Motel on North College Avenue, where the three of us and my one-year-old brother, Stan, crowded into the small space. I don't know what my parents did for home-cooked meals with no kitchen. I didn't care because we had a swimming pool in the front yard! Even though Stan and I were too young to swim, we were thrilled that our new home had its own swimming pool to dangle our toes in.

John and Audrie Bales owned the motel and kept a Shetland pony I liked riding on the property. The Bales nicknamed me "Wild Bill Hiccup." I've maintained an informal relationship with two of the Bales kids, Johnnie and Carol, to this day. There's something to be said about living with the same people in the same town throughout one's life.

L. G. joined us in Fort Collins in 1962 after retiring from Long-Bell. The chain of Everitt Lumber Yards was getting too large for Dad to handle alone, and the real estate development opportunities needed someone to seize the day, which Dad and Grandad were eager to do.

16

Papa

I enjoyed a wonderful life growing up in Fort Collins. Recalling all that made those years so fun and rewarding would be too self-indulgent. Besides, I now have a far more remarkable story to tell.

When my grandfather and grandmother moved to Fort Collins, I was privileged to spend more time with them, especially with my grandfather, whom I called Papa. Even as an adult, I used this endearing name for the dear man I loved. We could discuss anything and everything. He was always very encouraging. Like my father, Papa had a well-earned reputation as an honest and fair businessman and a thoughtful and generous person.

Like his own father, Papa was a large man with huge hands. He loved to laugh and eat! Each year there always seemed to be more of Les. Some people grow so large that they waddle when they walk. Papa was a waddler! Yet, this didn't detract from his charisma. In good humor, Papa would laugh with friends who often waved him on his way down the sidewalk with duck calls—quack, quack!

Papa continued to be my confidant and spiritual advisor until his death. His spirituality was semi-private but substantive. Although he never hesitated to declare his allegiance to Christ, he preferred to show his faith in wholesome speech, good humor, and generous deeds. I learned as much by observing him as by listening to him.

Papa died in April 1972 at the too-young age of seventy-one. His weight caught up with him, and a heart attack took him while at a business meeting in nearby Greeley. During his memorial service at First United Presbyterian Church in Fort Collins, Pastor Baird gave a eulogy that epitomized the Papa I knew: "His was a God-centered life. For, like a mariner on an ancient sea, Les always oriented himself in any situation with the prayer, 'Father, thy will be done in me.'"

In his closing prayer, the pastor said, "Father, occasionally it is our privilege to share a moment in time with one who makes life safe and secure, who gives to us the assurance that there are men and women of quality who rise above the commonplace and become uncommon men and women because they love thee more than anything else. We thank thee that Les Everitt was that kind of man."

It was a mystery to me where Papa's deep devotion to God originated. He was a sweet and wonderful

Christian man during all the years I knew him. There had to be a beginning to it all, but Papa never shared that with me.

Not until after his death.

17

Close Call

While attending college at the University of Colorado in Boulder, I occasionally visited my family in Fort Collins. As usual, the family business was progressing reasonably well, but I wasn't all that interested. My father and grandfather continued to grow and develop the various aspects of the enterprise, and all seemed fine until my grandfather died.

I wasn't expecting that!

Although there were many tasks to attend to, as there inevitably are when someone dies, my involvement was minimal. I was living in Boulder, attending school, and had just married the gorgeous Ann Arthur. Still, I felt terrible about not helping my grandmother during the days and weeks following the funeral.

One weekend, I drove to Fort Collins to help her sort through and move some of Papa's things. I then learned that some men like shoes just as much as women do. Papa must have owned five or six dozen pairs of shoes. He also owned some items that seemed rather odd to me, like a belt he wore under his pants with straps he attached to his socks to hold them up. I guess that was fashionable in his day. Go figure!

Papa had false teeth, and I found a couple of sets in special boxes along with various brushes and fluids to clean them. This was probably when I recommitted to a more regimented care of my teeth. I was not enamored with the prospect of having false teeth.

One afternoon, my Grandmother Memo (pronounced Meemo) asked me to clean out Papa's shirt closet while she ran a few errands. "Just stack the shirts neatly on the bed, David," she instructed.

"And David, there is a large cedar chest in the closet. Some of your grandad's new shirts from Hickman's Clothing for Men are there. Just pull them out and lay them nicely on the bed as well. Thank you, honey."

A word of warning about the beds and bedrooms of one's grandparents. When I was ten or eleven, I spent a few days with Memo and Papa while my parents were traveling. On the first morning, I searched for Memo; I had already said goodbye to Papa when he left for work.

I guessed the final place I might find her would be her bedroom. It was a large room with many interesting furnishings and a huge bed. She was nowhere in sight. Suddenly, I heard her in the bathroom and panicked. Yikes! What if she were showering or getting dressed and found me standing in her bedroom? Too far from the door to escape to the hallway, I quickly crawled under the bed without thinking of how I would eventually escape. *What if I'm not somewhere else in the house when she leaves her bedroom? Then what?* I was trapped!

My worst fears were realized when, from beneath the bed, I saw two naked legs going from the bathroom into the adjoining powder room between me and where she had just showered. I could hardly keep from shaking. *What if she finds me under her bed and thinks I'm watching her? Whatever you do, don't look, don't look!* I pleaded with myself. All my thoughts were horrific. *She's going to scream. She'll call Papa and my parents. They'll send me to juvenile prison. Peeping Tom, GUILTY! The rest of my life will be ruined!*

It seemed like it took Memo ten days to powder her nose, apply makeup, finally put on some clothes, and leave the bedroom. "David, honey, would you like me to fix you some breakfast?" she called loudly as she walked toward the living room.

I reasoned that I needed to leave the bedroom before she returned. I crawled out from under the bed and saw my salvation: The back bedroom door to the patio. Perfect! As quickly and quietly as I could, still shaking from head to toe, I went into the backyard, moved swiftly away from the bedroom window, and wandered around as casually as possible, hoping to get Memo's attention through the kitchen window.

It worked! My secret was safe.

"There you are," Memo said. "I've been looking all over the house for you. Would you like to come in? I'll make you breakfast."

May my grand *faux pas* serve to alert you to possible trouble anytime you happen near the bedroom of your elders.

18

Hidden Secrets

Just as Memo instructed, I transferred Papa's hanging shirts to the bed—he had a sizeable number of them, all very large. Then, I started on the packaged shirts in the cedar chest. As I removed the last shirt, I noticed a spider at the bottom of the chest scurrying along the back edge. I kept a close watch on it. I instinctively feared it was a black widow, but it wasn't. The spider hurried down a small hole and disappeared.

That's curious, I thought. I wondered where the spider went and if more spiders were concealed underneath.

I removed the last of the shirts and tapped the bottom of the chest. Sure enough, it sounded hollow underneath. When I pried up the false bottom, I discovered two leather-bound journals and a small white stone.

What are these? I wondered.

As I sat on the floor and started flipping through the pages of the first journal, it became increasingly clear that Papa had written these and did not want them to be found.

I was conflicted as to what to do. Should I show these to Memo or tell my father about them? Instead, I concealed the journals and the white stone in a box, put them in the trunk of my car, and took them with me until I could decide the best course of action. I feared that to disclose the content of Papa's journals during this emotionally stressful time following his death would be awful. I was initially disturbed by what little I had read. It would be cruel, I reasoned, to spring this surprise on everyone. It would only deepen the grief that Memo and my parents were already suffering.

After putting the box in my car, I returned to the bedroom and replaced the false bottom in the cedar chest—just in time!

"How did it go, David?" Memo asked as I was catching my breath. "Looks like you have everything in fine order. Thank you, honey. Stumble across anything?"

"Not really," I lied. "Just shoes, shirts, more shoes, and more shirts. What would you like me to do with this cedar chest?"

"Oh, I don't know. Maybe I'll find a way to use it. Or maybe I'll give it away. I never was very fond of that old thing."

On the return drive to Boulder with the contraband in the trunk, I decided not to tell anyone, including

Ann, about what I'd discovered. I talked to myself out loud, weighing the options.

"They say married couples aren't supposed to keep secrets from one another. That's probably important in most situations.

"But you're not sure telling her is a good idea, right? At least not now. You know it will be hard enough just to keep your mouth shut, let alone have her burdened with staying silent.

"You're right. Besides, if I tell her, she'll want to read what Papa wrote, and I want to read through the journals myself first. Maybe I can tell her later. In the meantime, where can I hide the journals?"

So much for my planning. A few weeks later, I decided that hiding the journals from Ann was useless. I was afraid she would stumble upon them, and I was also living with a feeling of guilt I could no longer ignore. Another advantage of telling Ann was the emotional comfort of not being the sole guardian of this information.

Ann skimmed over some of the reflections Papa had written during what appeared to be more than a year. She didn't have much interest at the time. On the other hand, I became fixated on gaining knowledge of everything Papa had written, hoping to understand the significance of the events revealed in these pages in our family's history. I also wondered if the journals contained material that would in some way impact my personal life.

I put my obligations to finish my degree at CU and to give Ann appropriate attention on hold. I had to read what I soon discovered were two volumes of Papa's reflections in one seamless story! Ann was generous and patient, affording me the time and liberty to indulge my newfound obsession.

19

Forest Canyon

eep in the high country of the Northern Colorado Rockies is the remote Forest Canyon of Rocky Mountain National Park. Atop its steep walls are the headwaters of the Big Thompson River. The 13,000-foot-high glaciers and water-soaked soils of the alpine tundra form the watershed of the Big Thompson, which flows eastward from the Continental Divide into the expansive valley of Moraine Park. From there, the river winds through the western foothills onto the Colorado plains. It eventually merges with the South Platte River on its course to the Mississippi River and the Gulf of Mexico.

Forest Canyon's floor along the river is mainly inaccessible throughout the year due to its remote location, rough terrain, and harsh climate. Its thick forest discourages access throughout its eleven-mile course except by bushwhacking on foot or leading a horse carrying supplies. As hostile as the environment is for humans, it provides a haven for wildlife, so a few resilient hunters and trappers periodically venture into the canyon during months when the weather allows.

Archaeological evidence suggests that several Native American Tribes lived in the mountains of Northern Colorado for centuries before European explorers discovered the Mountain West. Intertribal conflicts between Native Americans and Spaniards from Mexico occurred for decades in this region, with each party seeking to establish sovereignty over parts of the vast open spaces.

Government-sponsored surveyors and privately underwritten expeditions increased dramatically in Colorado, Wyoming, and Montana after the Louisiana Purchase in 1803. All were interested in finding this new land's resources and mapping trails into and through the Rocky Mountains.

John C. Frémont was perhaps the most notorious explorer of the bunch, conducting five expeditions between 1842 and 1854. Widely hailed as The Great Pathfinder, he gathered scientific and cartographical information while marking new trails from the Midwest plains through the mountains to Utah Territory, California, and the Northwest. The Cache la Poudre River, whose headwaters are less than a mile west of Forest Canyon, was frequently mentioned in Frémont's reports as a location where travelers stopped to rest before continuing north and west along the Cherokee, Oregon, Mormon, and Overland Trails.

20

No One
Goes There

April 10, 1920: At least I think it's the tenth, but I'm losing track of the day of the week, let alone the date. I guess it doesn't matter much except for trying to date these entries. I thought I would attempt to write down some of the stuff I see and experience in a journal to remember it later. I don't know how regularly I will actually do it.

Anyway, I don't know if I'd call it walking, hiking, or climbing, but I've spent the last several days finding my way into the park. I can tell I'm getting higher up. The days are pretty mild, but the nights are chilly. Most of the snow is gone except for some patches here and there. I see more and more animals, and the farther into the forest I go, the fewer people I see. I only saw one other guy far off today. Maybe I should head back to Estes, but something seems to be drawing me on. I'm so happy about all the new things I'm getting to see and experience. It's hard to explain. I'll probably continue for another day or so. I have plenty to eat, and the weather's great. The sky here is SO blue, and there are hardly any clouds. It's very different from Enid. I could see myself living here someday. But I do miss home.

In reading several initial entries in my grandfather's journals like the one above, I wondered how old he was when he came to Colorado and how his journals fit into what I knew of my family's history. When I did the calculations, I wasn't surprised that his journal entries matched the time of his extended hiatus after he finished high school and went to work full-time at the lumber yard. As I read further, it also became clear why he was so guarded regarding the details of his travels.

His initial excursion into Rocky Mountain National Park took him to the mouth of Forest Canyon. He surmised that trekking farther into the canyon would be impossible due to the narrowness of the gorge and the thick underbrush on both riverbanks. He wrote about reluctantly returning to Estes Park and weighing his options.

Talking to various people, he learned that the only possible route was to enter the canyon's west end at the headwaters of the Big Thompson. But everyone advised him that this was too dangerous. He recounted that people warned him, "No one goes in there except the Utes. For a greenhorn like yourself, odds are you'll never come back out. If a mountain lion or bear doesn't kill you, one misstep in that terrain could send you tumbling off a cliff. If you survive the fall, the beasts and birds will have you for supper. Don't do it!"

I figured Les, like most young men, thought he was invincible. He ignored the advice and found his way into Forest Canyon. What drove him could have been stupidity or testosterone, but his journal entries make clear he believed something was drawing him into this most remote part of Rocky Mountain National Park.

April 1920: I think my birthday is this week. I never imagined I would be wandering around Colorado on my twenty-first birthday. What a hoot!

I've heard about a trail by which I can drop into Forest Canyon from the top of the western side. It may prove risky, but something I can't explain makes me believe I'm supposed to hike into this wild country. Still, the nighttime noises in the forest make me nervous. How could I have been so foolish to think I wouldn't be an attractive meal for a mountain lion? The sound of owls haunts me as if they're saying, "Hoo are you? Hoo have you come to bother?"

21

The Accident

The farther Les descended into the canyon, the more isolated he was from civilization and the possibility of being rescued if he got lost, injured, or weathered out by unpredictable rainstorms or unseasonable sleet and snow. His journal entries indicate that, at one point, he became disoriented and nearly fainted from exhaustion. Navigating around, over, and through stretches of fallen trees and the thick willows began to take a toll. The springtime days were short; the sun was only visible in the canyon for a few hours each day. The nights were cool, and snow still covered large sections of the ground. With his food supply depleted, he began to consider the possibility that he could die alone in the canyon.

"It will take a miracle to get out of here alive," he mumbled to himself.

He lived on whatever plants looked edible and on repulsive grubworms and insects he found in rotted timbers. He even killed a snake and ate it raw, which made him throw up. He did his best to trek farther down the canyon, stopping to rest several times to recover his strength. At one point, he sat down, rested against a tree, and dozed off under the warmth of a sunny blue sky. When he woke up, he noticed something moving in the distance. Fearing it could be a dangerous animal, he sat perfectly still, hoping it would move past without seeing him.

When he glanced again in the direction where he sensed movement, he realized it was a young woman dressed like some of the Indian women he remembered living in Enid. He circled as quietly and slowly as he could to watch her. She seemed to be unaware of his presence. He scrambled atop a big rock for a better view and caught his left foot in a crack. He fell face-first and badly twisted his ankle. He might have also torn something inside his knee, but he didn't scream out for fear of being discovered.

His foot was firmly lodged in the crack. He couldn't move. His head was ringing, his face was bleeding, and his left hip was severely bruised, maybe even fractured. The pain grew as he wore himself out fighting to get free. His body began to shiver, and he thought he might be a goner.

As hope faded, a shadow moved over him. The woman he had seen stood over him. She had been watching him all along. Without speaking, she reached into the narrow split in the rock, untied the lace of his boot, and freed his foot.

Les screamed and nearly passed out.

"Do not move," she ordered. "I will return." She leapt from the rock and disappeared into the forest.

"Wait, who are you?" Les cried. "Where are you going? Come back!"

The woman soon returned and helped Les hobble off the rock and lie on a simple sled made of wooden poles and animal skins. When he was secure, she dragged him across a meadow. Although not a big person, she managed this with ease. She stopped to grab his backpack by the tree where he'd dozed off, then wound her way through the trees for several minutes until she reached a small cabin.

"Is this your cabin?" Les asked. He was still in pain, but no longer thought he was going to die. "Is there anyone else here?"

She ignored the questions and helped Les inside and onto a bed covered with woven blankets and animal skins. She gently lifted his wounded leg and made him comfortable. She wrapped his swollen ankle in a thin piece of leather, which stopped the bleeding, then shifted her focus to his swollen knee.

"Ouch! What are you doing?"

"Hold still," she said as she wiped the blood off his face. "Here, drink this." She shoved a wooden cup under his nose. "It will make the pain go away."

The warm drink stank and tasted awful, but the ache in his leg quickly diminished. Within minutes, he fell asleep.

22

Awinita

When Les woke after his first night in the cabin, he found himself lying on a more comfortable bed in a different room. Freshly cut flower petals were scattered on the blanket that covered him. He vaguely remembered the young woman helping him into the bedroom the night before, where he immediately fell back asleep.

Feeling slightly recovered, Les hobbled back into the cabin's main room. The woman who rescued him was not to be seen. He plopped down in a chair to ease the throbbing in his leg and surveyed the cabin as he sat in the morning silence. He made notes in his journal of some of the cabin's features. It appeared well-built. The main room contained a few chairs and small tables, which he assumed were crafted from trees in the surrounding forest. The walls were decorated with large animal furs. There were also several brightly colored blankets hanging on the walls and lying over the backs of chairs. Various flowers in small clay vases were set on the tables and windowsills. Larger bunches of flowers were placed in buckets on the wooden floor. What appeared to be a handful of bear furs covered the floor in various places. The beauty of this rustic cabin deep in Forest Canyon surprised him.

When the young woman returned, she set a cloth bag on the table, washed her hands in a large stone basin, and came to sit beside her surprise visitor.

"How do you feel?" she asked in a pleasant, soft voice. "How is your leg?"

"It still hurts a lot, but the throbbing in my foot isn't too bad. I think whatever you gave me to drink has helped with the pain."

Les was able to focus on the young woman's appearance for the first time. She had changed into a skirt and a buckskin top with colored beads. He imagined she had dressed this way for his sake. She had long coal-black hair, honey-colored eyes, and smooth brown skin. She was quite pretty and relatively young; he guessed she was in her late teens to early twenties.

"What's your name?" Les asked. "How old are you? Are you living alone? Where are you from?"

She just smiled and attended to the bandage around his ankle.

"My name is Les. What's your name?" he asked again.

"Awinita." She paused, then added, "In your language, it means 'little deer.' What does the name 'Les' mean?"

"I don't know for sure."

He tried to say her name, "'Ah-wee-nee-tah.' Thank you for rescuing me. You saved my life. Do you live here alone?" he asked again.

Awinita laughed at the way Les pronounced her name. They both relaxed and chatted comfortably for the next hour. Later, Les reflected in his journal how Awinita seemed both a young, inquisitive girl and a mature, self-assured lady. He found her gentle and firm. He described Awinita as more fascinating than any other woman her age he had ever met.

Les told her how he'd come to Estes Park and found his way into these mountains. He mentioned how scared he'd been, yet how he felt drawn to explore the canyon. After elaborating on his journey, he asked Awinita to tell him her story.

She shared her childhood memories of living in Forest Canyon and what she'd learned from her parents about how the three of them came to be there. "Mother was full-blood Cherokee of the Deer Clan. She lived in Indian Territory near Arkansas. Her name was Laniyah (LaNEE-yah). It means 'a Light that is found within.' Mother grew up in a place where both Whites and Cherokee lived as neighbors. Father was of the Keetoowah Band of Cherokee Indians, born of the Wolf Clan.

"Keetoowah keep the traditions of the Old Settlers," Awinita explained. "Among our people and many Whites, Father was known as Ben Slow Walker. Mother told me Father had deep thoughts and prayed to Creator (UNELANVHI) when he walked, so he walked slowly.

"Father reminded us that he saw more of what He Who Dwells Above wanted him to see when he walked slowly. He believed that a slow walker has more time to discover the heart of all Creator has made and also more time to search for what is in his heart, and in the hearts of others. He and Mother met at a Baptist Mission Church on the plains of Indian Territory, where both English and Cherokee were spoken. There, they learned of Creator's Chosen One, Jesus, and his love for all people. The Sacred Traditions of the Keetoowah and the Word of the Great Storyteller and his Message Bearers all tell of the same good road the Chosen One has called all people to walk with him."

Awinita's English was surprisingly good, Les thought.

"Mother told me she liked how Father looked," Awinita went on. "He was a very handsome, honest, and peaceful man. For my father's part, one night, he told me of the first time he met Mother. He said he liked her beauty and kind spirit. He thought she was very wise. Because Mother was Cherokee but not of the Keetoowah Band, she did not know Keetoowah traditions and customs when they first met. Some storms surrounded their being together.

"In time," Awinita continued, "many in the tribe grew to accept her as she adopted more of the Keetoowah ways. Still, a dark cloud remained over her in the eyes of some, especially among those who were part of the Nighthawk Society, who wanted to stay with the old ways. Mother was educated by Whites, and this knowledge left some anxious."

"So, you are part Cherokee and part Keetoowah?" Les asked, somewhat confused.

Awinita sat up straight. "I am Keetoowah. My clan is the Deer Clan. Keetoowah is the tribe's original name. Later, some adopted the name Cherokee. My family has kept the name of the 'Real People'—Keetoowah."

"How long after your parents married were you born?"

"I do not know. Mother told me only where I was born."

"Where was that?"

"A town called Enid, in Oklahoma Territory. They lived there for a short time, and then we moved here soon after I was born."

"I was born in Enid, too!" Les blurted out. "In 1901!"

Awinita stared into his eyes and said, "You lie."

It took Les some time to convince her he was telling the truth. When she finally believed him, she began to weep quietly.

"So, now we are both here," Awinita said, drying her eyes. "How can this be? Both born in Enid, and now together in this place. We have come by different paths to be here. Is this of the Great Spirit's choosing?"

"Well, I'm not sure I believe all that," Les said. "I think it just happened by chance. But still, here we are."

"All things of chance are shown in time to be from He Who Dwells Above. The Great Way Maker knows how to draw chance into the best paths for human beings."

23

On the Run

Les's strength steadily improved over time as the pain and swelling in his leg lessened. He helped with chores around the place as best he could, but his mobility was still limited. His left hip hurt markedly whenever he attempted to walk more than several yards. He thought about heading home, but knew it would be foolish to try walking out of the canyon by himself in his condition. His memory of how he almost lost his life hiking into the canyon was still fresh. The thought made him shiver.

Besides, he was enjoying his time with Awinita. In one of his journal entries, he mentioned how intrigued he was with the whole experience. "I want to know more about her. I mean, how unusual to accidentally come upon an Indian girl living alone in this place. I can't decide if I'm attracted to her because of her beauty or how mysterious she strikes me, being here alone."

One spring day, Awinita was gone from the cabin for most of the morning. Les puttered around, trying to be helpful. When she returned, she prepared something to eat from items she had gathered from the garden next to the house. It was like porridge, which she called "sofgee." Awinita served tea made with dandelion root and succulents from a prickly pear cactus. Les thought it tasted pretty good, but missed his usual morning coffee.

As the two ate, they talked. Les was curious to learn from Awinita why her parents came to Forest Canyon. Initially, she had been unwilling to talk about it, but he broached the subject again. He saw in Awinita's face an uneasiness; something grieved her about this part of her history.

"Why did your parents choose a place as distant and secluded as this?" Les asked.

"A man in Enid named Jenks hated Father," Awinita began. "Jenks had a bad heart. He hated all people with skin not his color. He said Father killed his baby boy. It was a lie. Jenks made many others in Enid hate Father. They would not sell groceries or supplies to Mother or him. Some wanted to kill them. Mother told me Jenks wanted me dead, too, since he thought Father killed his baby. He wanted revenge. We left Enid to go somewhere they could not find us. Mother told me the man's broken ways made his heart grow bad. When we left, Mother said Jenks and his friends chased us. They wanted to kill us. I was just a baby."

"But why did your father choose this of all places?" Les wanted to know.

"A tribal elder with medicine told Father to go to a Vision Quest site called Old Man Mountain that guards a deep canyon in Colorado. Slow Walker learned that several tribes had come to this sacred spot for many ages to get visions and learn about their futures. They smoke, pray, and fast for days. Here, the Great Spirit tells them what they want to know. Father brought Mother and me to Old Man Mountain from Enid to learn where we should go to be safe. Creator showed him that this canyon was to be our home. It was a place far from the changes brought about by the settlers. Here, Father said, we could follow the ways of the *Ani-Yun'wiya*, the 'Real People.' It was a place to teach me truths learned from our Keetoowah ancestors and from the sacred teachings of the One sent by God, *Tsi-sa* (Jesus), and his Twelve Message Bearers, who speak about the People of the Way. These writings, too, speak of Creator's Real People. This was why we came to the canyon. It has been a place for us to live in peace with Creator. The Old Seer told Father that one who would be a great teacher among the Keetoowah would come from his seed."

Les wanted to ask her where her father and mother were now, but Awinita wished to change the subject and learn more about him. They went outside and walked down a path in the woods. Les had to go slow.

Awinita put her arm in his to steady him. He told her about his family and his life growing up. She was interested in what kind of town Enid was, and about places like schools and stores. She wanted to know what a lumber yard was.

"What games do White children play?" she asked.

Les realized she had never lived in a town, had friends her age, or had any neighbors. Their lives had been so different!

When they returned to the cabin, it was getting dark. Les was tired and in some pain. They briefly held hands and then went to their separate rooms for the night. Awinita had moved Les into her father's bedroom the night he first came to the cabin. She slept in what had always been her room.

Les's journal entries made it increasingly clear that he and Awinita grew more comfortable with each other as time passed. He wrote about them teasing each other and laughing together. When they talked about their former lives with their families, they sometimes cried together and held one another for comfort. They confessed they were occasionally lonely and often felt scared of what might happen in the future. They were becoming friends in an extraordinary way.

24

Oginalii

A s the days passed, Awinita and Les sat together, and she shared more of her family history to answer Les's persistent questions.

"Where are your parents now?" he asked.

"Mother walked on two winters past," Awinita said. "She was sick for many seasons. Her body grew weak, so it was good for her strong spirit to go live with *Tsi-sa* in a new body and place, a place very near but beyond what we now see and understand completely. Father told me once that Mother was old in wisdom yet young in spirit. Father missed her dearly."

"Mother taught me many things about the Great Spirit," Awinita continued. "She was wise in the teachings of our tribal ways and the wisdom of the Chosen One's Messengers. She and Father learned from tribal elders in their *Tsu ni la wi s di* (church) how both traditions agreed on many things. Mother was a great teacher in her church. Many Whites and Indians, both men and women, sought her wisdom. Do you see those books on the shelf over there? They belonged to Mother. She carried them with her when we left Enid. She studied many things each day."

At this point, Les interrupted. "But I didn't think the Cherokee religion was the same as the Christian religion."

"Not all Keetoowah believe the same as Slow Walker and Laniyah, who bore me, but many do. We see *Eloheh* (harmony) between much of the Keetoowah tradition and the Sacred Teachings of Creator found in the Bible. Mother taught that many religious symbols, ceremonies, and creeds may give us a glimpse of the truth beyond them, but they are not the clear truth.

Awinita rose from her seat and invited Les to join her in front of four windows, two flanking either side of the front door. As she pointed to each window, she explained:

"When traditions, teachings, and ceremonies are not dirty, pitted, or badly formed, they are glass-in-the-wall through which we can see what is real beyond them. They may wake up something that has been asleep in us." As she touched two separate panes, Awinita continued, "If stained or fractured like this one or that one, they can easily lead us astray.

"Creator Sets Free (Jesus) said, 'I am the Great Spirit's pathway, the clear truth about who Creator really is, and the life of beauty and harmony he offers to all. There is no other guide that can take you to the

Father.' What we read in the Sacred Teachings about the Chosen One, his life and teachings, are the clearest glass-in-the-wall."

Awinita opened the door and motioned for Les to follow her, saying, "Yet, *Tsi-sa* invites all human beings to move beyond their glass-in-the-wall and walk out-side with him into what is real. He has said to us that he is the Door and he is the Truth."

Les frowned. "So, you believe all religions point to Jesus?"

"No, I do not. Religions can point the way to the true Creator, or lead astray. When you go to the river and gaze upon it, you see your face if the water is clear. Traditions, ceremonies, and creeds can either dirty a stream or they can wash away the gook so the water may reflect your face more clearly. The Great Spirit shows followers of Tsi-sa what is murky water and what is clean."

Awinita stopped talking and sipped the drink she held in her hand. Then she put her hands on Les's face and quietly added, "The greatest sorrow is when human beings choose not to gaze into the river at all."

Les was anxious to hear more. This was a new way of thinking about religion for him.

"In Mother's Bible, I learned the truth from Small Man, who your people call St. Paul. He taught follow-ers of Creator Sets Free in his time: 'For now we only know some of the story, but the time is coming when we will know the whole story from beginning to end. For now, it is as if we are looking at a poor reflection in muddy water, but then we will see face to face. For now, my knowledge is full of holes, but when that time comes, I will know the Great Spirit as well as I am known by him.'"

Les was impressed that Awinita could read her mother's Bible. When he told her so, she replied, "Before Mother walked on, she taught me these things as she showed me how to read English. Each morning, I sat with her and Father, and we would read from the Bible and tell stories about Creator's love for all people."

As Awinita talked to Les, he picked up the Bible on the table and noticed the cover identified it as a Native Indian translation written in English.

"Some mornings," Awinita continued, "we would also pray and sing and dance. On warm mornings, we would sit outside to be close to Creator in what he had made. We sang the Cherokee Morning Song:

We n' de ya ho,
We n' de ya ho,
I am of the Great Spirit, Ho!
I am of the Great Spirit, Ho!
We n' de ya ho,
We n' de ya ho,
I am of the Great Spirit, Ho!
I am of the Great Spirit, Ho!

Ho, ho, ho, ho
He ya ho he ya, Ya ya ya
It is so, it is so.
Great Spirit, Great Spirit, Great Spirit

"As I grew older," Awinita continued, "I learned to speak and read the Whites' language and understood better how they lived. After Mother walked on, I began reading her Bible and her books. Some of my favorites are the writings of a Scottish man named MacDonald. When I was a child, Mother read his fairy stories to me. I still find wisdom and beauty in his stories. They improve my trust in *Tsi-sa*. Mr. MacDonald once echoed the desire of *Tsi-sa* when he wrote, 'You must do what you can to know me, and if you do, you will. So that I may, I seek to know him more and more each and every day.'"

After they finished lunch, they went outside in the sun. Awinita helped Les to a grassy spot and spread out a blanket. Once comfortable, they continued talking. Awinita missed her mother as she spoke of how they were constant companions.

"She taught me the ways of Creator, about all he had made and the ways of human beings. Mother was a good teacher in many things. We often walked together in the woods to pick nuts and berries. 'These you can eat, but these you cannot,' she would tell me as she pointed to different plants and mushrooms.

'Boil this flower with this bear root and drink. It will take away your pain and make you well.'"

Awinita and Les sat silently for some time, listening to the forest. A sense of peace blossomed between them and their surroundings: the clouds in the blue sky, the chirping birds in the distance, the trees stretching awake—all of it.

"And what of your father?" Les asked. "Why is he not here?"

Pointing to the west, Awinita said, "Father would often leave the cabin in the morning and slowly walk this path into the woods. He told me this was his time with the Great Spirit to learn what Creator would tell him. Mother and I were not to follow. One morning, I disobeyed Father and followed him. When I came to a certain spot, I saw that he had climbed high into a tree, looking in every direction as if watching for something or someone. When I told my secret to Mother, she told me that Father believed the Great Spirit had told him to protect his family, so he watched each morning from the highest tree to learn if danger was near. 'You should not follow him again,' she told me.

"One day, Father told me he was to go to the valley towns before the snow came. He did not say why he was going. Still, he has not come home."

"How long ago did he leave?"

Awinita just shook her head. "He walked away during the Trading Moon, ten moons after Mother walked on. We say *Du-ni-nu-di*; you say October. He has not returned. I often count the small plates on the turtle's shell to tell me how long it has been. Eight moons have passed." Tears welled up in her and Les's eyes.

After a long silence, she said, "I talk too long. Tell me more about you. Why are you here?"

"Because I wanted to explore places other than where I was born and raised," Les answered.

Awinita looked at his bandaged leg. "You will not explore much for some while."

Les smiled. "I guess you're right." He felt awkward asking, but he didn't have much choice. "Is it okay if I stay here until I can walk better? I'll help you around the cabin any way I can."

Awinita agreed, and they made their way back into the cabin.

Over the next several weeks, they got to know one another better. They respected each other's privacy in the small cabin. Les helped the best he could. Awinita would often be away for long hours. When left to himself, Les would take long naps or read one of Awinita's many books. He even flipped through her mother's Bible now and again, curious.

Most days ended with conversations near the fire. One evening, Awinita told Les his name would not do. "Les is not a good name for you here," she said as she placed a small white stone in his hand. "This stone will remind you of your new name. On it, the Great Spirit has engraved another name that, in time, only you can see, just as was written in the Bible's last words—The Book of the Great Revealing—'I will give the mysterious bread to the ones who win the victory. I will also give them a new name carved into a white stone. A name known only to the one who receives it.'

"Where you come from, your name is Les. To me, you will forever be *Oginalii* (O-gee-Na-Lee). It means, 'He Is My Friend.' You alone will know this name among your people. The white stone is for you to remember me and to remember to trust *Tsi-sa*."

25

Native Genius

As early summer warmed the canyon, Oginalii spent much of his time helping Awinita tend her garden. He became increasingly helpful as time and patience healed his body. While working in the garden, he came to appreciate how knowledgeable and resourceful Awinita's father, Slow Walker, had been. At first, Les had been so self-absorbed in his desperate circumstances that he overlooked Slow Walker's true genius. The man's workmanship in transforming a trapper's old, dilapidated cabin, which he and Laniyah discovered in the canyon, gave witness to an engineer's intelligence and an artist's skill.

"Father told me he learned how to build things when he worked beside men from the church back in Oklahoma Territory," Awinita explained one morning. "During their early years in Forest Canyon, he built furnishings from wood and stone. He also worked with the shed antlers from deer, moose, and wapiti, which are cast to the ground each year.

"Father taught me to respect all creatures. When we hunt for food, we honor what we kill. We do not take the meat only and leave the remains to rot. Creator gives his people each portion of our animal brothers for helpfulness. Their spirits go on with us as we go on after they are killed. Look with the eyes of your spirit and you will find our forest friends still with us in their bones made into tools and spoons, their tongue, heart, and marrow, which we eat to build our strength, their sinew and intestines for our bowstrings, and for binding things together. Every day, we walk through all of this and remember the sacrifices made so we can live."

Les was beginning to understand better the sacred way the Keetoowah approached life. He wondered if he would come to see life as Awinita did.

"Father gradually added to the cabin walls the furs he and Mother skinned from bears, foxes, beavers, and big horn sheep for insulation to ward off the winter cold and summer heat," Awinita explained. "Wooden shutters on the outside of the cabin keep out drafts and let in light through the windowpanes he made from the thin sheets of mica nature had provided in abundance in the canyon. He expanded the hearth of the stone fireplace and padded it and the seats of the chairs with beaver pelts."

"It's nicer than many people's homes back in Enid," Les said.

One morning, while working beside Awinita in the garden, Les became conscious of the extraordinary engineering features that Slow Walker had designed and built into his family's forest home. He penned the following journal entry:

Summer, 1920: One day, after Awinita and I had planted seeds in the dry ground, she went to the garden's edge and dug a shallow trench with her heel. It quickly filled with water to moisten the soil atop the seeds.

"Where did this water come from?" I asked in amazement.

"Come with me," Awinita said. "You will see."

I did my best to keep up as she walked into the forest toward the river. We soon arrived beside a small pool covered with mist from an underground thermal spring. From it, a crude tree-bark-lined trench had been built that led to the cabin. It provided warm water to wash with and to turn winter ice into drinking water. It was so well constructed into the cabin's walls and kitchen counter that I had not even noticed it before. How could I have been so dense?

"My people use these warm springs for their healing water," Awinita said. "There are many like these in the canyon and beyond. Some tribes consider them sacred and go to them for rituals."

She showed me a second trench above the hot spring that brought cool water to irrigate the garden and fill a large stone basin inside the cabin for cleaning and drinking. There was no need to haul water from the river every day. I was humbled. My prejudiced thinking toward Indians was demolished. No longer did I see them as ignorant or without resources.

It was during this time that Awinita taught Oginalii the native practice of Listening to the Land. "The White Man 'tells' the land what to do for him; what to grow for him, how much to grow, and when to grow it. But the land will not be told for long what to do before it will resist the Whites' ways and won't obey. If we but listen to the land, she will tell us what fruit she will bear before she is barren. Humans cannot force their ways upon her. My people have learned how to respect the land and the rivers, and all created things. If we listen, we will learn to live in the beautiful harmony the Way Maker has designed. Our God is an artist. This is what we have come to learn. This is what Creator desires every man to learn."

26

Born to Be Free

One evening, Les was alone in the bedroom reviewing several of his earlier journal entries. One entry reminded him of a conversation he had the morning he found Awinita relaxing in one of her favorite places in the cabin, where she often sat alone. There, she enjoyed the sun's warmth as it greeted her, sitting in the bay window her father had crafted. She was reading from her mother's Bible, as was her morning habit.

"What are you reading, Awinita?" Les asked as he pulled up a chair.

"The words of Creator Sets Free, whom you call Jesus, about living free," she replied.

"I'm living free!" Les said confidently. "I don't need some human being or invisible deity to tell me what to think, say, or do. From what I can tell, the Christian God is a dictator, not a fan of freedom."

Awinita smiled and asked some odd questions. "Are you not a human being? Do you not tell yourself what to think, say, and do?"

"Well, sure, but I'm free to choose what will make me happy."

Still smiling, Awinita challenged him with an idea about freedom he had never considered. "For you to make choices is not freedom. Unless you make good choices, you will not be free. You will not know a good life. You will be a slave to your bad choices. It is so with all human beings."

She saw Les's uncertainty and continued to talk, expressing herself with her hands and words and explaining that true freedom—true happiness—comes by choosing Creator's true path. She put her finger on an open page in her Bible and read Way Maker's words: "If you walk in my footsteps and follow my teachings, you will truly be my followers. Then you will see and understand the truth that sets all people free" (John 8:31–32).

"But no one knows the truth," Les protested. "Everyone decides what the truth is for themselves."

Awinita continued to express herself strongly. "Can you choose to float in the air like a feather? Can you decide to be a horse or a snake? Lies cannot be made true by believing they are true. The Great Spirit's truth cannot be passed over if we are to live the good life Creator has made for people to live. God, who knows all, has created the good life to live because of his love for all people. He has revealed this good life to us and invites us to trust that this is so and walk in this path of light. All who do will be free, free from ruin and sorrow. Hear what *Tsi-sa*, the Way Maker, said when he walked this earth: 'Thieves enter only to take away life, to steal what is not theirs, and to bring to ruin all they cannot have. I have come to give the good life, a life that overflows with beauty and harmony' (John 10:10).

"The freedom and truth you speak of," Awinita added, "leaves a man with only a shallow happiness. Pleasures from his desires soon fade away and steal away permanent things."

As she again turned to her mother's Bible, Awinita read what Way Maker told his earliest followers: "I am the Great Spirit's pathway, the truth about who he really is, and the life of beauty and harmony he offers to all. There is no other guide who can take you to the Father. To know me is to know my Father" (John 14:6–7).

"If his words are true, freedom comes when we know him and his ways," Awinita said. "In friendship with him, we learn what is true, what has been true from the beginning. Oginalii, are you wiser than he who made you? We are truly free when we learn we are not free."

"But why do I still doubt what you tell me is true, Awinita?"

"Do not be afraid of your doubts, my friend. He who truly doubts thirsts for what is true. This is good doubt. Good doubt will help you find the truth, and so doubt becomes a doorway to faith if opened. Unopened, his trust remains lost in his own understanding, drifting from one doubt to the next. But when he who doubts opens the door and crosses over into the light of day, Creator Sets Free greets him, and doubt is traded for trust."

Awinita reached out, touched his hand, and smiled. Then, she stood and invited him to join her for a morning meal.

Several entries in Les's journals reflected how he often sat silently, pondering the new ideas Awinita challenged him with. He wondered if this young woman he happened upon deep in the forest of the Colorado Rocky Mountains was some kind of sage. Her manner and words seemed both extraordinary and compelling. Had he been told that such a woman as Awinita was here, he would have doubted its truth. But now, his experience was slowly washing his doubts aside.

27

A New Way
to Pray

"Do you talk with Creator, Oginalii?" Awinita asked one evening when they were sharing a meal.

"Well, when I go to church on Sundays, I close my eyes and pray with everyone else. And I always bow my head when my father says grace before dinner. Sometimes, when things go bad, I ask God to fix them. I don't know if I believe he will. I don't know if there is a God who answers prayer. Do you pray, Awinita?"

Awinita explained how her mother had helped her understand prayer differently. "Mother told me not to say prayers but to talk with God. She encouraged me to find time to be alone and ask him to teach me what it is to pray. 'If you ask him this,' Mother said, 'you are praying, for you will be talking with God. He will talk back to you with his answer.'"

Les was confused. "But I was taught how to pray at my church and at home. Are you telling me this is not prayer?"

"Do you talk with God in these prayers of yours, or are you just making words?"

Les wondered if most of his prayers were prayers at all. He had to admit that God was rarely on his mind when he prayed as he had been taught.

Awinita went on. "When I first asked Creator to teach me to pray, his Spirit said, 'Write to me what your heart wants me to know and listen for what I want you to know. Just wait and listen with your heart. Be patient. Pay attention. Talk with me with your pencil and write down all I tell you.'

"Oginalii, the Great Spirit told me that praying means to listen more than to talk. We can talk with him in many ways: in words we say, in songs we sing, in wordless thoughts, and in writings. The Chosen One listens to the longings of our hearts and our gratitude for the joys of our lives that we experience together with him. The writings of Small Man to the sacred family in all nations tell us these things as I find them written in Mother's Bible: 'His Spirit talks with our spirit and tells us we are his children . . . helping us in our weakness, for our prayers are often empty words. But Creator's own Spirit groans deep within us, without words, making our weak prayers strong. The one who sees into our hearts knows the Spirit's thoughts and prays with us in our weakness so we can become who he created us to be'" (Romans 8:16, 26–27).

Les's journal reflected this conversation with Awinita and how he began experimenting with prayer by talking with God in some of his entries. Over time, he found himself talking with God on many occasions throughout the normal course of his days. Sometimes he walked and prayed. Sometimes he sat still. His journal entries gave the impression that prayer was becoming less an event and more of a constant drumbeat pulsing behind each moment of his life.

28

It's about Time

The longer Les stayed in the cabin, the more he lost his sense of time. His pocket watch had been broken in the fall that injured his leg. When Awinita first brought him to the cabin, he asked what day it was. She brought him an old turtle shell and showed him the twenty-eight plates on the shell. She explained the Keetoowah way of marking time.

"The plates around the edge of the shell mark the twenty-eight days of the moon cycle, while the center design of the shell has thirteen larger plates showing the thirteen moon cycles of a year." She pointed to one large plate and then a single smaller one along the edge of the shell and told Les that day was number seven of *Guyegwoni*—the Ripe Corn Moon. "According to the White Man's calendar, this is July when ears of corn are first roasted."

Counting hours of a day seemed peculiar to Awinita. When Les showed her his damaged watch and explained its use, she took it in her hands and inspected it.

"How strange. A little gold machine tells you when the day begins and ends, when to do this or to do that. Is it one of the gods you obey?"

At first, not having a watch frustrated Les. Ultimately, he found a kind of freedom in living without having to measure his life as he'd been raised. Watches, calendars, and schedules became meaningless in the canyon. Awinita measured life by significant events and the natural cycles of nights and days, moon phases, animal mating and birthing periods, phases of her physical growth, and seasons of the year. She distinguished one day from the next by how many sleeps had passed.

Gradually, Oginalii focused less on the future and more on the present. He and Awinita's days were woven together with threads of work, play, rest, and conversations. When he explained his new way of thinking about time to Awinita one evening over dinner, she shared what she had learned from Laniyah before she died.

"Each morning, Father, Mother, and I ate together. Afterward, I would sit with Mother in the big window. We would let the sun warm us. I would listen to her read from the Sacred Teachings. She wanted me to learn the ways of Creator. I remember the morning she taught me some things about how time goes. She read to me what Stands on the Rock wrote that I was not to forget."

"Who is Stands on the Rock?" Les Interrupted.

"The Whites call him Peter. He wrote, 'With the Great Spirit, there is no difference between one scute and one thousand winters. So then, our Honored Chief is not slow in keeping his promise, even if some see it that way. Instead, he is being patient with you.'

"'God is in no hurry,' Mother told me. 'Neither need we be. Your father, Slow Walker, understands this.'"

Awinita shared a second passage she remembered her mother reading for her: "'Do not worry about tomorrow's trouble. It is enough to trust Creator to give you the strength you need to face today.' The One Above Us All holds each part of the day in his hands. He will meet us there when we arrive. We do not need to worry about the future.' I have remembered these teachings. Do you understand, Oginalii?"

She didn't wait for an answer but invited him to sit with her in the big window. She picked up the Bible from a stack of books beside her, found the book of Ecclesiastes, and read aloud: "'God has made every-thing beautiful for its own time. He has planted time without an end in the human heart, but even so, we humans cannot see the whole of God's work from beginning to end.'

"What does the Great Spirit say to you about time in these words, Oginalii?"

"I'm not sure. May I take Laniyah's Bible to my bed tonight and read this part again? It may be something for me to understand."

"It is for you to have as long as you desire." Awinita smiled as they stood. "I believe God is waking something up in you that has been asleep."

That evening, Les studied the readings and reflected on their meaning regarding time. Even as his eyes closed in sleep, his mind wrestled with all his new thoughts.

When he shared his confused thoughts with Awinita the next day, she said, "Oginalii, now you are beginning to see something in a new way. All is not as it first seems. Humans have their own time. God, too, has his time. They are different, but humans live in both times at once. You will soon learn it is the same with more than just time. What is true and real is not to be understood by thoughts alone. Creator gladly gives his Spirit to all who come with a pure heart and follow the Chosen One's right ways, so human beings can understand the beauty and wonder of all things with their new eyes.

"Oginalii," she added with a smile. "No longer will I think of you as 'Small Eyes."

29

The Utes and Climbing Bear

O ne August morning, Les pushed aside the shut-ters of his bedroom window to see, in the new-day sun, a group of Indians camped in teepees several yards from the cabin. There were six men, one woman, and two pack horses. He was alarmed by their pres-ence. He had seen no humans apart from Awinita in the canyon before.

His first instinct was to find Awinita and tell her about the trespassers. Then he saw her sitting with the Indians and talking with the woman. She seemed com-fortable with the Indians. When Awinita saw him peer-ing out the window, she motioned to him to join her.

Les got dressed and hesitantly approached the group.

"Oginalii," Awinita said, "sit with us and greet my friends." She pointed up the valley. "These are Utes from the White River that flows beyond the mountains where the sun sleeps. They stop here during this sea-son, time after time, when traveling from their village to trade for supplies in Estes Park and with people of the valley beyond. Their horses rest near our clear water."

Awinita turned and pointed downstream. "The canyon grows too small for a horse to pass that way. The coming of the Utes to this place has been so for as long as I can remember. These also are oginalii, 'friends.' We will see them again when they return to their home. They will leave some supplies with us for the winter."

The leader stood and introduced himself to Les. "I am Black Hawk. Why are you here?"

Les explained briefly about his accident.

"We, too, found this place by accident." Black Hawk told Les about their discovery of Awinita and her parents in the canyon several years before and how a kinship had developed between them. "Even though we are of different tribes, that does not matter. Creator has for us to live in peace with these Keetoowah and to care for each other."

At this, some in the group murmured in their language. Awinita explained to Les that they were wondering who the White man was. She told them his story, and they welcomed him, greeting him by his new name, Oginalii. In time, everyone broke away from the vanishing fire to tend to the horses and prepare to break camp—everyone except Awinita, Black Hawk, and Les.

Black Hawk questioned Awinita as Les listened.

"Where is Climbing Bear? We did not see him in his tree."

Awinita began to weep. "I do not know," she sobbed. "Father left during the Trading Moon for the valley towns, promising to return after only a few sleeps. He has not come back. I fear he has walked on to be with Mother. Still, I wait for his return."

Awinita told Black Hawk the sad story of her father's disappearance, the same story she'd told Les. Then she explained to Les why the Utes had named her father Climbing Bear. It was for his habit of climbing trees to learn of possible dangers coming their way from afar. He reminded the Utes of a bear up in a tree. Whenever the tribe traveled through the canyon, Climbing Bear would spot them from a tall tree and wait for them to pass beneath him. They would greet one another, and Climbing Bear would accompany them to his cabin. In the Ute tradition, a bear is known as a protector and messenger. Slow Walker happily adopted the name Climbing Bear from the Utes as a second name because of this belief.

The Utes always enjoyed visiting Climbing Bear's family, and the stop served as a good resting place on their journey to the Colorado Front Range and back. They took advantage of the therapeutic hot springs near the cabin whenever they passed through the canyon.

When Awinita, Black Hawk, and Les finished talking, Black Hawk called for the woman in their group to join them. He told her about the death of Awinita's mother and her father's disappearance. He said they would visit Awinita more often, and the woman would come along each time for company. He pleaded with Awinita to join them when they returned to their village over the ridge, but she refused. She wanted to remain in Forest Canyon to be there when her father returned.

Black Hawk asked the woman to stay with Awinita in the canyon until they returned in seven days.

The woman's name was Halona, which in English meant "Happy Fortune." She slept on the floor by the fire, wrapped in her blanket, and proved to be a quiet but helpful guest.

30

Deer Clan

On a late-summer morning, Les rose early to find Awinita gone as expected. His leg was still sore, but he could put more weight on it with the help of a walking stick she'd made him. He decided to venture farther out to test his knee and ankle. Until now, his outside activities had been limited to walking near the cabin with Awinita.

On this particular day, the air was warm, and threads of sunlight dressed the trees. The heat had awakened a hatch of feather-like flies that danced like fairies playing tag on the sunbeams. He decided to take a walk through the woods. He came to a fallen tree, where he sat to rest his throbbing knee. He saw Awinita seemingly talking with a young deer in a nearby clearing. He watched this meeting for several minutes until Awinita and the deer parted ways. He tried to understand what he'd just seen.

At supper, he brought it up. "Awinita, I took a longer walk this morning. As I rested on a fallen log, I noticed you talking with a deer. Did my eyes deceive me?"

"No, Oginalii," she replied. "I saw you, but I could not turn to you. The deer was lost and frightened. Not many whitetails live in this valley. She was looking for her family and asked for my help."

"What do you mean? Animals don't talk!"

"I am Deer Clan," Awinita said, "as were my mother and grandmother. This is why I was named Awinita. It means 'Fawn.' Creator made our clan to give care to deer. This whitetail came to me to learn where her herd might be. I directed her there."

"So, you believe you and the deer can understand each other?" Les asked skeptically.

"God gives voice to all his creation to speak in different ways by his Spirit. We may understand if we have ears to hear. Did Balaam's donkey not speak to him in a language he understood? Does your dog not respond when you call him? Do you not recognize his bark warning you of danger? So, the deer speaks to me, and I understand."

"This I can hardly believe," Les protested.

"Do you believe I am talking to you now?"

"Of course."

"Why do you believe this to be true?"

"Because I recognize what you are saying, and you understand what I say to you."

"It is the same with the whitetail and me. We

understand one another. This is why I believe it— because it is true."

Les dropped the subject. No good would come from arguing the point. He was not convinced, yet something he couldn't explain had gone on between the deer and Awinita.

31

A Good Day
to Dance

L es wrote in his journal about the many late summer and early autumn days he spent wandering the woods to enjoy the sun's warmth while waiting for Awinita to return from her daily walks. He often took a now-familiar path to a clearing near the noisy river swollen by runoff trickling down the canyon walls into the Big Thompson River. On one occasion, he saw Awinita reclining barefoot in the hollow of a small boulder, staring into the air with a soft song on her lips. She appeared to have been writing some things in a notebook lying on her lap. The meeting was so memorable that he attempted to summarize it in his journal:

Fall,1920: I quietly approached and sat on the grass beside Awinita, gently slipping off my boots, careful not to disturb her. Some moments later, she spoke.

"Isn't it beautiful, Oginalii?" she asked without turning to look at me.

I tried to follow her gaze to see what she was looking at. She raised her arm and pointed. "There."

"Do you mean that stand of aspen trees?"

"Yes, and all else from here to there and all around the trees. Isn't it all so beautiful? Do you hear the birds in the branches? Can you see the reflection of sunlight upon the golden leaves, which will be quaking in the breeze in just two moons? Is it not a delight that Creator has painted three white clouds in the blue sky above to greet us? Does it not fill your heart with joy, Oginalii? Isn't it beautiful?

"The Great Spirit reveals the mystery of who he is through what we see, hear, feel, taste, and smell," she said. "I came this morning to join my beautiful brothers and sisters in singing praises to Creator for such wonder. It gives our Maker much Joy to gift all humans with such joy!"

Awinita went on to explain, "Is it not written in the Sacred Teachings that Creator has made himself known to all human beings in all things he has made? Are we not invited to join with all the beauty of the earth in rejoicing, 'For you shall go out in joy, and be led forth in peace; the mountains and the hills before you shall break forth into singing and all the trees of the forest shall clap their hands.'"

Once she had finished speaking, Awinita rose and took my hands in hers. "Here," she said. "Dance with me, Oginalii. Just as my ancestors danced, and as King David danced before the One Above Us All to celebrate Creator's love. Come now, dance with me!"

Awinita sang songs in her native tongue as we danced and laughed. I had not danced with a girl since high school. It was a good day to dance!

32

Work and Re-creation

During the evening, after dancing in the woods, Awinita and Les returned to the cabin and enjoyed a meal near an open fire. Les appeared to be somewhat distracted as they ate. When Awinita asked him about it, he confessed that what she had led him to discover profoundly impacted how he perceived nature and perhaps all things.

Their extended time together had matured into a closeness they both enjoyed. They had grown accustomed to calling each other by the endearing names of Awi (Aw-ee) and Ogi (O-Gee).

"Awi, I never thought God might have enjoyed gifting humans with what he created," Les said. "I took it all for granted; it was just nature. But to see it the way you do as a personal gift from God is something new, and I think I like it."

Awinita smiled. "What you discovered today, Ogi, is only to dip your toes into the shallows of the stream. Creator desires you to walk with him into the Deep. As

163

written, 'Deep calls to deep at the roar of your water-falls; all your rapids and waves come over me.' Soften your heart, Ogi, and you will learn that it is not what you look at but what you see."

Les pondered the implications of their conversation, and a few days later, asked, "Awi, in your tribal ways, are we to leave what Creator has made just as we find it? That doesn't seem practical. I see lumber for building houses and making furniture, where you see only beautiful trees. Where you delight in the sound of wild birds gobbling and the aroma of wild onions, I imagine a turkey dinner like my mother always fixes on special days."

"When Creator made human beings," Awinita explained, "he invited us to find pleasure in all he formed and to care for it as a mother would care for her child. Our Great Father, who has imagined and created it all, also allows us to imagine and craft many things ourselves. We can create from what he has supplied in nature, so we might be delighted as he is in our creating the objects of our own imaginations and skills. This is the meaningful work Creator calls us to do—re-creation for our further joy, so that by our work, others also will prosper. In all of this, Creator is made happy."

Awinita paused to make sure Les was following her.

"Ogi, it is the work of The Great Father's hands *and* our own hands that we are invited to enjoy and respect. In our tribe's tradition, when we take the life of a living thing gifted to us by Creator, we honor the sacrifice made by taking not only the meat of a *wapiti* for nourishment but also its antlers to craft into tools and furniture and use for art and medicine. We cover our floors and walls with the hide for warmth and beauty. We tan it to make leather for clothes. The *wapiti's* sacrifice means his life surrounds us each day. It is the same as Mother learned from her church about the sacrifice of Creator Sets Free and how he shares his life with us beyond his death."

As Les considered this idea, he realized that this very belief energized his family in the lumber business. Perhaps his and Awinita's families derived this divine work ethic from the Bible. He recalled a verse he had heard preached about at church: "There is nothing better for a man than that he should eat and drink and enjoy his work. This is from the hand of God; for apart from him, who can eat or have enjoyment?"

33

Going to Water [Ama]

all, 1920: I woke up this morning and found Awi missing from the cabin. She's an early riser, but she usually returns by mid-morning. Once she returns, it has become our habit to share a morning meal while we read and discuss something from her mother's Bible. She hadn't returned today, and I was beginning to worry. The sun had risen well above the horizon, and the air was warm. I put on my boots and walked down the river trail to see if I could find her.

I knew she sometimes went to the river to sit near the warm pool. I saw her as I neared the water and pulled back the willow branches. She was bathing. She was naked! I stayed back so I wouldn't startle her, but I didn't turn away. I must admit, my heart began to pound as I gazed upon her beautiful body. She was lovely!

At last, she stood in the shallows and dried herself with her hands, then began walking toward me, water still gleaming on her skin. I froze! She did not stop walking my way when she noticed me in the willows. She fixed her eyes on mine and smiled. I'm sure my face was bright red with embarrassment. She wasn't ashamed or uncomfortable at all. When she got close to me, she picked up her buckskin dress, draped over a nearby branch, and slipped it on.

"Did you come to find me, Ogi?" she asked in her typically sweet way.

I told her I was worried that something terrible had happened to her.

"I am fine. Here, sit with me, and I will explain."

We sat on the grass near the stream, and she told me about a Keetoowah tradition.

"My people have a ceremony called 'going to water.' It is a sacred ritual to wash away sickness and bad thinking. It is like the Christian baptism, but we go to water often, not just once. I come on many mornings and on the first day of each new moon, as I used to do with Father and Mother, to pray and sing songs to Creator who meets me here in ways his Spirit has prepared for me. I listen when he tells me what he wants me to know. The voice of the waters speaks to me of Creator's never-ending love for me. Maybe you will come with me with the next new moon, Ogi."

Although Les didn't join Awinita in the water ceremony each day, he did join her with the coming of the next new moon. As they bathed together, they prayed a traditional Cherokee prayer she taught him:

"May your hands be cleansed that they create beautiful things. May your feet be cleansed so they might take you where you most need to be. May your heart be cleansed so that you might hear its message clearly. May your throat be cleansed, that you might speak rightly when words are needed."

34

A Secret
Way Out

During Les's stay with Awinita, they often discussed the contrasts between the city life he knew and the life in the wilderness familiar to her. Les did his best to convince her there was much to offer in a settled community, as he'd learned from growing up in Enid. He expressed his desire for her to return to Enid with him to live. Awinita was adamant in her resistance to the idea. Her parents had convinced her that it was in Enid that the pressures to abandon the traditional Keetoowah life in harmony with nature and contrary to Creator's ways were at work. Furthermore, she imagined that all towns were decadent and had nothing to offer her. Besides, she still believed Slow Walker would soon return to her in Forest Canyon.

A journal entry in late autumn contained an idea Les hoped would break the stalemate between them about her moving from Forest Canyon:

Fall, 1920: I know the Utes will return through the canyon to trade in the towns along the Front Range in the next several weeks and that Awinita trusts them. I want to convince her to ask them to take us with them so she can see the energy and goodness of the townspeople and the resources they have to create a full and meaningful life. It hurts me to think that Awinita would spend the rest of her life alone and lonely. I hope that both she and the Utes will agree.

After serious discussions, Awinita finally agreed to go when Les suggested she might learn something about her father's whereabouts from the townspeople.

When the Utes arrived, Black Hawk agreed to let Awinita and Les accompany them on the round-trip to and from Estes Park and Fort Collins, where the Utes made camp and traded for supplies for their winter settlement near Grand Lake.

Les was excited about giving Awinita a taste of the town life he had known. He was also curious to learn from the Utes about a route out of the canyon that didn't require climbing back the way he first entered from the headwaters above. They knew a secret passageway that the townsfolk he had talked with before his journey into Forest Canyon knew nothing about.

The hike out of the canyon was not easy. Most of the way, the Utes followed a path in or alongside the river. Les figured the journey during the spring must have been particularly dangerous due to the turbulence created by the runoff into the river. But this trip had plenty of its own challenges. The deadfall of tangled timbers, branches, undergrowth, as well as large boulders, required slow and strenuous progress as the party bushwhacked their way to the mouth of the canyon. Once on the meadowlands in a moraine beyond Forest Canyon, the Utes set up a crude camp in the dark, craving rest after their exhausting journey.

Les took mental notes of the route as best he could until they reached the place where Black Hawk had blindfolded him and Awinita to keep the secret passageway hidden from others. Still, Les tried to listen for clues on how he might find this secret doorway out of Forest Canyon someday.

Awinita had never been to a modern village, let alone a town like Fort Collins, with a population of about 9,000 in 1920. Estes Park was a year-round home for about 300 people. Les described Awinita's first reaction to these two communities as shocking.

Fall, 1920: Awinita held tight to my side as we walked the dirt streets, dodging the horse-drawn buggies and flatbed wagons. She was both frightened and curious. Downtown Fort

Collins was particularly noisy and crowded; everyone hurried to who knows where. The look on her face made it clear that she was disturbed by all the commotion. More than once, she asked if we could return to her cabin.

In Estes and Fort Collins, I asked as many merchants as possible and others who might know if they had seen an Indian named Ben Slow Walker. Awinita asked people the same question. No one had seen or heard of them, although a Fort Collins bartender said three foul-looking strangers had asked about an Indian named Slow Walker not too long before. "They seemed hell-bent on finding him," he told us.

After three nights sleeping by the Poudre River east of Fort Collins near the Council Tree encampment, the Utes were ready to return to the mountains. Les and Awinita were beyond ready to go back themselves. They had talked about their impressions of the trip, but neither was prepared to reach any conclusions. They both wanted more time at the cabin to process their thoughts and emotions.

35

Winter in the Wild

Winter can come early in the high country of Colorado. Heavy snowfall in Rocky Mountain National Park makes extended time spent above 8,500 feet risky. The winter of 1920–21 seemed exceptionally long to Les, who was not accustomed to such harsh conditions week after week, month after month. Life with Awinita took on a whole different rhythm. Outdoor activities were limited to trapping rabbits and squirrels to eat, chopping wood, clearing snow and ice from the roof, and a few short excursions into the woods to enjoy snowshoeing on those exceptional days when the air was crisp and still, the sky bluer than blue, and the only sounds were an occasional crying eagle above the snow-flocked trees.

Awinita maintained her morning ritual of "going to water" in the river's thermal pool. Les would join her on the first day of every new moon. The new moon excursions, at least on one occasion, were extended beyond the usual ceremonial washings and prayers.

They swam together in the warm water, lingering in the pool and talking as the steam rose from the surface. When they climbed out of the pool, they stood shivering in the cold air, hugged one another, quickly dressed, and hurried back to the cabin's warmth.

Winter days in the canyon were short and dark. Awinita and Les spent much of their time indoors, talking and tending to chores. Despite being confined in the small cabin, they gave each other the space to be alone. When Awinita returned from her daily river ritual, they ate breakfast, read from Laniyah's Bible, and shared their thoughts about spiritual things for the balance of the morning. Although he had grown up in the Presbyterian Church, Les now had to ponder ideas he had never heard of before, or at least didn't remember hearing. One such conversation found its way into Les's journal:

Winter, 1921: This morning, Awi and I read a piece of the Bible written by Small Man, her name for the Apostle Paul. He spoke of something she's been trying to explain since I came to her cabin. "Humans without the Spirit cannot see all things revealed by Creator. Some things seem foolish and are beyond their understanding. Those walking with the One Who Sets Free can know the meaning of all things in ways those without Christ do not understand. We are they who understand the mind and heart of the Great Spirit and can sit in council with him."

Awi read a second verse, this one from the Gospel of John: "One must be born of both water and spirit to walk Creator's good road. The human body only gives birth to natural life, but it takes the Spirit of Creator to give birth to spiritual life."

She then asked me if I was born this second way. I told her I did not know of this mystical birth. My heart began to pound as I thought of this experience. As I sat alone in my room writing about these things, I wondered if this was something God had for me to experience. I still have so many questions, but now I am asking myself if the answers come only after I have this second birth Jesus spoke of.

Les's skepticism about Christianity gradually diminished the longer he lived with Awinita. In her words and behavior, he recognized a distinction between a religion with beliefs about Christ and the living relationship with Jesus that Awinita possessed. God became more personal to him and less of an object of discussion. But this experience with God remained elusive and inconsistent at best. Les recalled being haunted by something Awinita told him she had heard from a Keetoowah chief who himself walked the good path of the Great Spirit's Chosen One (Jesus). "It is possible to be a Christian and follow Jesus, but it is very difficult."

Just as the chill of early morning gives way to the warmth of the day, so Awinita and Les's relationship moved from suspicion through caution to attraction. They became increasingly fond of each other through the long months. They would often sit and talk after their evening meal, wrapped together in a blanket in front of the fire. They recognized that a decision about their futures was inevitable. Their love for one another was tempered by the reality of the clashing cultures and different locations they each called their home.

"You can't live here alone, Awi," Les would argue. "From everything we have read in Laniyah's Bible, Creator wants his people to live in a community."

"But Ogi, if you stay, I won't be alone. We can make our own community and live in the traditional ways of my people. I can't go with you. I must wait for Father to return, or I could lose him forever. Won't you stay with me?"

The thought of Slow Walker never returning to Forest Canyon or his coming back only to find Awinita gone left her weeping in Les's arms.

"But what of my family?" Les asked. "My mom and dad are waiting for me in Enid. I have friends, a job, and a whole community to return to. Everyone will love you if you come home with me. It will be a full and exciting new life for you. I can't stay here, Awi. My heart will die."

Journal entries traced how Les and Awinita repeatedly discussed their predicament without resolution. By the time winter finally melted into spring, little remained to say about their futures. They each had prayed for wisdom according to their traditions. They even prayed together, hoping for a third way.

It was not to be.

36

Wolves

Since arriving in the canyon, Les had frequently listened to the distant cry of what he guessed were wolves. One late-winter evening, he asked Awinita about their haunting howls echoing off the canyon walls.

"What you hear is the cry of coyotes," she explained. "Both grey wolves and coyotes live in these woods. Both are predators, but they are not the same. If unprovoked, the wolf attacks and kills only to eat its prey. Coyotes are known at times to attack and kill only for sport, playing with the wounded, then leaving the uneaten to die and decay after growing bored with their entertainment. Their way is evil. The Trickster has twisted the coyote's heart."

Some months later, Les had a chance to meet a wolf for the first time. He and Awinita were out for a walk early one evening to enjoy one another's company in the beauty of the fading light. Suddenly, Awinita stopped and put her finger on her lips. A lone wolf was blocking their path. Even after it saw Awinita and Les, the wolf stood its ground. The couple left the trail to find an alternate route to avoid the animal. The wolf also moved, continuing to impede their progress. When they returned to the main trail, the wolf trotted a few yards down the path, stopped, turned, and howled.

"*Wa-ya-ni*. She is calling. She wants us to follow her," Awinita whispered.

And so, they did. The wolf led them off the trail and into the woods, turning at times to see if they were following. Before long, they heard voices and slowed to listen. They stopped atop a large outcropping of rock, then spotted three men camping streamside in a small clearing. Their oily leather coats and pants were torn and filthy. One carried the fur of some animal over his shoulder. Another wore a stupid-looking hat. Les could barely tolerate how they all stank, even at such a distance.

"Seth, gather some wood and start a fire. I'm gettin' hungry. Burl, go shoot something. Got to be squirrels or rabbits out there somewhere."

A few minutes later, Burl came back with a wild turkey. He plucked it partway, then tore out the chitlins and set everything on the hot coals.

"Throw me that bottle so I can wash these chews down," the older man said.

"Here ya go, Pa."

Pa answered with a loud, long belch.

All three laughed as they competed to see who could burp and fart the juiciest.

Awinita whispered, "If we had stayed on the trail, we would have stumbled into their camp."

Les nodded in agreement. "How did they get here?"

Like a shroud, the river's noise allowed the two spies to remain undetected as they continued to listen.

"Damn Injuns! I hate 'em all!" Pa's face turned bright red in the firelight. "Who do they think they is, trying to become Baptists, Methodists, and the like, so as to fit right in. Hell, they ain't no more Christians than Lucifer himself. They're as pathetic as them niggers. But boys, if we find these three savages, they're dying, yah' hear? 'Vengeance is mine, sayeth your Pa.'"

He took a long swig from the bottle, then wiped his mouth on his filthy sleeve.

"That bastard, Slow Walker, killed your baby brother! Nearly destroyed your Ma. She still grieves mightily. Now we'll take him out, along with his kid and her mother. It's only right. An eye for an eye, and a kid for a kid, just as the Good Book tells it."

The youngest brother, Seth, jumped to his feet, grabbed his crotch, and piped right in. "I'll have my fun with the kid if we find her. Then off she'll go to her Happy Hunting Grounds."

Sinister laughs echoed off the night walls.

"Boys!" Pa barked out. "Slow Walker is mine! Let's torture him good before I slit his throat. Or maybe we'll just hang the bastard and watch him jerk and twitch till he's limp as a danglin' sausage over an open fire. Same color as a sausage, ain't he? What could be more fair than a slow death for a Slow Walker?"

More repulsive laughter. Then, Pa turned to his eldest son. "Burl, guess that leaves the old squaw for you. Think you can handle her?"

"I never rode a squaw before. Think she might bite?" Burl fell down laughing.

"I almost had a piece of her once back of the Long-Bell lumber yard, but some good-doer kid chased me off." Pa, whose name was Jenks, relished the memory and eagerly anticipated what he considered his rightful due.

The three men snickered and made crude jokes as they passed the bottle of moonshine around.

Seth suddenly looked in the direction of Les and Awinita. "What was that?"

"Aw, son, you're spooked. Just some animal snapped a twig. We'll blast whatever wild thing moves our way."

It wasn't long before the three passed out for the night.

"We need to get out of here," Les whispered, taking Awinita's arm. She was frozen in place, stunned by what she had heard. Les pulled her away. "Let's go."

They quietly slipped into the darkness, careful to avoid stepping on dry brush, fearful of waking the marauders. The wolf appeared and led them back to the cabin, walking slowly through the woods, pausing at times to let them catch up. It was as if the animal could sense their worry and watched over them as a canine would her pups.

Once Les and Awinita reached the cabin, the wolf disappeared. Safe for now, they were still distraught.

"I can't sleep," Awinita said. "What if they find their way here in the morning?"

"I don't know what's best," Les admitted. "We can leave the cabin, but where would we go? We have bows and arrows, but they have guns and outnumber us." Then his good judgment kicked in. "Let's stay here for now and keep watch. When our nerves are settled, we can come up with a plan." To himself, he admitted, *This is the most scared I've ever been!*

No one came their way that night or the next day. Two mornings later, as they gathered food from the garden, Awinita stopped working. She looked around, then glanced at Les and said, "Someone has died."

"What makes you think so?"

Awinita pointed at an owl glaring at them from a tree branch several yards away.

Once the owl had their attention, it flew away.

Without a word, Awinita ran after it. Les was close behind. The owl guided them to where they had seen the three malicious men camping a few nights ago. Two of them lay dead on the ground. It was clear a pack of wolves had torn them apart. The clothes had been ripped off their bodies; their flesh had been eaten. Blood was everywhere. Their hearts had been torn from their carcasses and tossed aside to rot in the sun.

The third outlaw was nowhere to be seen.

"These were wicked men," Awinita murmured. "They were coyotes making sport of murder. Their poisoned hearts grew toxic through the years from holding so much hatred."

Later that evening, Les reinforced why this terrifying encounter should be enough to convince Awinita to leave the canyon with him: "It's too dangerous for you to be here alone. What if your father never returns? What will you do?"

Awinita dropped her face into her hands and wept. She was conflicted. *What should I do?* she asked as she petitioned her Creator.

37

Back to the Garden

Les and Awinita had reluctantly surrendered to the reality that he would depart the canyon alone. In anticipation of the inevitable, they engaged in activities that would prolong their time together. Summer meant a new growing season, so their last days together were preoccupied with tending the garden for what they hoped would be a bountiful harvest. The tasks at hand filled the space that would otherwise be spent in fruitless conversation about how they might still be with one another.

Les did include one conversation from that summer in his journal that he thought was meaningful.

Summer, 1921: "Ogi," Awinita said. "Gardening together these last few days makes me think of Creator's beautiful garden we will someday live in beyond the end of time when he makes all things new. I wonder if we will know each other then."

"I don't know, Awi. I like the thought, but I'm still not sure of what happens after we die. Will people with dark hearts like those men from Enid, who wanted to kill you and Slow Walker, also be made new?"

Awinita paused, then replied, "Ogi, I know just this: Only those who shut love out will be shut out from love and left to die howling in their own darkness. It is a dark heart and broken way that destroys a man, not Creator."

"I hope you're right, Awi. I hope you're right."

Les grew pensive as he pondered the state of his soul. "God," he prayed, "please chase away any darkness in my heart by the light of your love I've now learned more of."

38

Sweet Sorrow

They knew it would be their last night. Les would walk out of Forest Canyon with the dawn. Ogi and Awi had gradually fallen deeply in love during their time in the canyon, yet neither would turn their back on the life they had inherited. Her home was in the canyon; his was in the city. Few words were spoken during their last supper. Quiet tears painted their faces in the flickering candlelight. The food was left untouched as emotions spoiled appetites.

"I love you, Awi."

"*Gv-ge-yu-I,*" she replied in Cherokee. "I love you, too."

They settled together on the bear rug before the fire, resting in one another's arms. Days before, they had exhausted conversation about possible paths keeping them together. Their hearts were already broken. More talk would only bring more pain.

"Will I ever be able to hold you close again?" Awinita whispered.

Les answered with gentle kisses on her cheeks, lips, and shoulders.

In the end, they abandoned themselves to unrestrained passion and intimacy.

Earlier that year, a solar eclipse and a total lunar eclipse were visible in the sky over the western United States. It was an old belief that the sun and moon were lovers who came together during an eclipse for a brief time before going their separate ways in the sky. It was as if heaven itself gave witness to Les and Awinita's romantic eclipse. Like the sun and moon, they must go their separate ways to fulfill their destinies.

The next morning, Awinita saw that Les had enough food and water for his journey home. She accompanied him to the porch, where he asked her to sit with him one last time on the bench Slow Walker had made; a spot they had shared on many occasions. It was an excuse to postpone his inevitable departure.

Les had been thinking about some token he could leave with Awinita to remember him by. Months before, she had given him the small white stone the day she had blessed him with his new name, Oginalii. Now, he pulled from his pocket the silver dollar his father had given him.

"Awi," he said as he placed the coin in her palm, "my father gave me this silver dollar the day I left Enid as a token of the love he and my mother sent with me.

He bought it the year I was born to express their thanks-giving and affection for me. I didn't know of this coin before my trip here. When we said our goodbyes at the train station, Father said, 'May this silver dollar be a reminder that your mother and I are with you, though separated by many miles.'"

Les reached into a side pocket of his backpack and showed Awinita the white stone she had given him to remember her by.

"In exchange for this stone, I give you this coin so you might never forget me. It symbolizes what I've gained by being with you these many months. On its face is Lady Liberty. She reminds me of you and the true freedom you are helping me discover. Father told me these words, *E pluribus unum,* mean 'Out of many, one.' I believe we have become one, Awi.

"And see, on the backside," Les said as he flipped the coin. "It's a bald eagle who watched over us during our time together and will watch over you in my absence. In his talons are the arrows with which you taught me to hunt. He also holds an olive branch to remind you of the peace you have helped me find. See the words above the eagle's head. These are the most important: 'In God We Trust.' You have shown me what it means to trust Creator and walk in his path. When you remember me, know I go now to learn how to live my life trusting the Way Maker whom I have come to know while being with you. May this silver dollar remind you that I am with you still, though separated by many miles."

After a kiss and prolonged embrace, they stood and stared into each other's moistened eyes for the last time. Les turned and walked into the woods. He imagined Awinita standing on the porch, crying until he disappeared. He hid his sorrow by not looking back.

Both perseverance and good fortune were required for Les to successfully retrace the Utes' path out of the canyon. At times, he wondered if he would make it out alive. His heart was already broken; maybe it would be fitting if his life came to an end in this place. Later, he wrote in his journal about a passage from the Bible he and Awinita had talked about many times: "Creator decided ahead of time when and where each tribe would live. He did this so that all people could look for him and find the trail that leads to him. Creator is not far away from any one of us. It is through him that we live, walk, and have our being."

39

Journal's End

In Papa's final journal entry, he detailed how he tarried in Estes before traveling back to Enid. He described the confusion he felt about leaving Awinita alone in Forest Canyon. "Have I made a mistake by leaving?" he wrote. "Should I have stayed with her until Slow Walker returned? The Great Spirit would not abandon her, would he? Does God want me to return to be with her? I'm so uncertain as to what I should do."

In the end, Papa hurriedly returned to the canyon, unsure what difference seeing Awinita again would make. He wrote, in part, about what he found.

July 1921: As I made my way back to Awinita's cabin, I noticed it appeared unkempt and hurriedly abandoned. My stomach was overcome with emotion as I imagined what I might find inside. Horrible thoughts ran through my mind. When I entered the cabin, it was mostly as it was when I left, except it was clear that Awinita had moved out. I darted around, looking for a clue about where she might have gone.

As I was leaving the cabin, I noticed a scribbled note attached to the back of the door.

Ogi, know I am safe if you return and find me missing. Even though I miss you, it was right that you returned to your life in Enid. I will never forget you, and I know you will always remember me. I will tell people you are my friend—my Oginalii. And know this, the Great Spirit has assured me, 'Oginalii is also my friend.' Creator's own Spirit goes with you, before you, behind you, beside you, above you, beneath your feet, and within you. *Gv-ge-yu-I.*

Awi

Overcome with emotion so deep it hurt my heart, I pulled the note from the door, went to the bedroom that once was mine, and cried myself to sleep clutching the note in my hand. The next day, I started my trip out of Forest Canyon by myself a second time and then on to Enid, where I now write what I suspect will be the last entry in my journal. I am at peace. I am confident Awi has found her good path. Now I must find mine.

It had been roughly fifteen months since Les set out from Enid to explore the mountains of Colorado. Upon his return to Enid, he found things nearly as he left them. However, he was not the same person as the young man who had ventured off the year before.

Despite his easy reintroduction into Enid, he frequently found his thoughts in Forest Canyon. A heavy spirit of remorse crept into his heart on occasion as he questioned if he should have left Awinita alone in the forest. He asked God to forgive him, not only for leaving but for allowing his affection for her to drift into a sensual desire that brought them both further than what they knew in their hearts to be best. At times, these thoughts brought tears as he lay on his bed in Enid.

In time, he would come to grasp the forgiving love of Christ lavished upon him, which freed him from the guilt associated with this and all his failings. One of Papa's favorite passages of Scripture, which he always carried with him in his pocket, was the sixteenth verse from the first chapter of John's Gospel: "For from his fullness we have all received grace upon grace."

40

Now What?

After turning the last page of the second of Papa's journals, I leaned back in my chair, hoping that by this simple change of posture, the hundreds of thoughts running through my head would be sorted out. I remember being numb as if exhausted from taking a final exam after cramming for forty-eight hours straight.

As the present moment came back into focus, I was confused about what to do with the secret journals. For now, I would just put them in the bottom drawer of my desk and answer that question in due time. I had to return to my studies. Semester finals were coming up in just a few weeks.

41

Good, Bad, or Ugly

I was once asked, "Would you say your life has been good, bad, or ugly?" My answer today is the same as when I was first asked: "Good." Actually, I would say, "Great!" Not that there haven't been challenges along the way, but on the whole, I would have to compare them to zits in junior high: a bother and an embarrassment, but somewhat incidental and quickly forgotten.

Even before moving to Colorado from Enid, my parents loved spending time outdoors. After the move in 1953, they indulged themselves in an abundance of activities the Rocky Mountains had on offer: hiking, camping, horse-packing trips, fly fishing, bird hunting, snow skiing in the mountains, along with water skiing, golf, and tennis with friends in town. Fort Collins was relatively small, just under fifteen thousand people, but the presence of Colorado State University and a rapidly growing population of young families meant that sporting events and cultural and social activities were abundant.

While Mom tended to my sister, brother, and me, Dad worked hard to make the Everitt Lumber Company successful. Not only was he a hard worker, but he was also smart. He was well-liked by virtually everyone, regardless of their station in life. It would require a separate book to recount all his accomplishments, which included multiple successes and awards, as well as leadership positions in the military (Bronze Star), business (Colorado Business Hall of Fame), civic life (Community Builder of the Year), and even politics (State Board of Agricultural). If asked what he was most proud of, he would quickly reply, "My wife Joyce and our whole family." He was exceptionally good at being just who he was.

Dad occasionally invited me on business trips to other towns where he and Papa owned lumber yards. He said he needed me to count pieces of lumber for the annual inventory. I suspect it was his way of keeping me out of trouble with my friends and out of Mom's hair. I'm not sure it worked very well on either front.

My parents subscribed to a philosophy of child-rearing that established clear guidelines as to right and wrong alongside a long-leash approach to monitoring the day-to-day activities of their three kids. At least, that was my experience. I'm not sure that they trusted Stan, Claudia, and me as much as they trusted God to watch over us. All in all, he did. Yet, there were times when I was excited about pushing the 'good behavior envelope.'

When I was four years old, we lived on the busiest street in Fort Collins—College Avenue—across from the Spudnut Shop, which made the best donuts for miles around. Because I was in the habit of rising quite early in the morning, I would regularly venture out of the house well before daybreak, run across College Avenue, and knock on the donut shop window. The owners, making the day's donuts rise with the sun, would unlock the front door, sit me down in one of the booths, and put the first donut of the morning run in front of me, along with a cup of hot chocolate. I think I was their most regular customer!

When finished with my early breakfast, I would run home and quietly sneak back to bed before my parents got up. I would have continued this stealthy routine for months if it weren't for my dad finding me out when he came for a donut and a cup of coffee to take on an early morning road trip.

"David! What are you doing here? Get home right now, and don't you sneak over here again, you understand?"

"Can I take the rest of this donut with me?" I pleaded.

"Not to worry, Bob," Gus, the owner, told my dad, attempting to calm him down. "David comes over here quite often, and we watch out for him. He's a good kid. Always asks lots of questions. He's fun to talk with first thing in the morning."

Because we lived next door to a college fraternity during those years, I was made an honorary member. I learned the secret handshake and was educated by my "brothers" in the activities and practices of the fraternal ways. I suspect I was the youngest Alpha Tau Omega fraternity member in the United States.

When I was five, our family moved to 1000 W. Laural St. across from CSU. Here, I made some good friends during my early grade-school years. I won't mention full names, but some of the guys I hung out with taught me things my parents never did. Jay, for example, taught me how to smoke when I was seven. His dad often asked Jay to buy him cigarettes at the nearby gas station. With the money he gave Jay for the errand, he and I would ask for two packs. We felt justified in keeping one for ourselves as a delivery fee. As long as his dad received a handful of change and his cigarettes, he remained oblivious to our business transaction.

Jay and I would find various venues to indulge in our newly acquired activity. We were so sophisticated! One afternoon, we were short on time, so we could only get as far as the neighbor's truck parked in the street before needing to satisfy our newly developed craving. Unfortunately, the old truck's seat was ripped, and some ashes set the stuffing on fire. We had both talked about wanting to grow up and become firemen, but we found our skills wanting on this occasion, and the whole truck went up in flames!

We escaped and hid behind the corner of a house across the street to watch the police and firemen put out the fire. Not until my sixties did I confess to Jay's younger sister that we were the arsonists. She was shocked! I drive by the crime scene every so often just to remind myself of God's grace lavished upon delinquents such as me and Jay.

Although my parents never learned how the fire started, it wasn't long afterward that, during dinner one night, Dad thought it a good idea to bring my propensity to smoke to the attention of the whole family.

"David, I understand you have taken up smoking. Since we don't smoke, why don't you show us how it's done?" He tossed a pack of non-filtered Camel cigarettes across the table. "Give it a go, son; smoke the whole pack to give your brother and sister a good lesson."

I was terrified, as you might expect, but quickly enough let everyone around the table know that earlier this very day I'd decided to quit smoking. There was little conversation during the rest of the meal. Hard for any of us to transition into regular supper-time discussion after that. I'm happy to report that I honestly did give up cigarettes at age seven.

As I approached adolescence, I discovered unconventional ways to make some money. I peddled Coke and popcorn during rodeos held at CSU and supplemented those wages with whatever money I could find under the bleachers. I would have gladly returned the cash to the fans who unknowingly let the money fall from their pockets, but finding the rightful owner was virtually impossible, so I considered the coinage lost and found. After all, possession is nine-tenths of the law. On one occasion, my daily compensation amounted to nearly fifty dollars.

Still in grade school, I collected hundreds of glass soda bottles from the construction site of Lesher Middle School. I routinely exchanged the glass discarded by the workers for cash at the grocery store. Each time I pulled my red wagon home, piled with bottles, Mom would drive me to the store to complete the transaction. She never charged me for the transportation. I've always thought that my most useful class at Lesher was Economics 101, which I attended even before the school was operational.

I was involved in every sports activity I could find time for during primary and secondary school. I played almost every team sport: football, basketball, baseball, swimming, wrestling, track, golf, and tennis. I joined the fencing club in college and traveled throughout the state to poke fun at our competition. I fell in love with the mountains and spent every free weekend hiking, skiing, fishing, or hunting. On several occasions in high school, I ventured into the mountains alone or with a friend or two, hiked into a secluded spot, and set up a tent for a few nights.

I was only called to the principal's office once in grade school, once in junior high, and twice in high school. I did get arrested once while in college, but I never had to spend a night in jail. I never did discover why someone I didn't know shot at me a couple of times, or others beat me up on the streets of Boulder while attending CU.

In later years, I dabbled in cliff diving with my brother, parachuting, spelunking, mountain biking, cycling, competitive fencing, scuba diving, river rafting, and snow caving with a couple of buddies. I enjoyed rock climbing in the foothills near Fort Collins and Boulder. I found inspiration in the challenge of mountaineering in the U.S., Europe, South America, and the Himalayas, along with some professionals who have climbed many of the tallest peaks in the world. However, I would classify myself as a "wanna-be" in this regard.

Overall, I would characterize my life during these years as adventurous and mischievous. In hindsight, I would suggest that God had something better in store for me and kept me from falling off the edge, literally and figuratively. I embarrassingly take responsibility for some years of reckless adventure and foolish mischief. Yet, I have no doubt it was God who graciously countered my stupidity, allowing me to survive. It would soon become clear that he had an even better and more profound happiness waiting for me than I already enjoyed. His idea was a grander adventure and a tempered mischief.

42

What about God?

So, what about God?

I think it was around ninth grade that I began to question my own religious beliefs. Witnessing my parents' faith, I couldn't deny their high moral standards and positive approach to life. They were exemplary in every respect. Well, except Dad was all thumbs, spending as much energy trying to button his shirts as he did changing a tire on the car. And Mom, she had a fetish about men remaining free of facial hair, especially my brother and me. Otherwise, they wove their religious convictions seamlessly into their lives.

Despite growing up in the Christian Science Church, it was the beliefs of the religion that I struggled with. I would relentlessly ask my mom to answer my 'if, then, why' questions: If God is real, why doesn't he show himself? If God is good, why is there so much that is bad in the world? Etc.

Mom's answers didn't satisfy me. In fact, they left me with even more questions. I attended Sunday services less frequently. Once I was off to college, I stopped going altogether, except with my parents when I was home for Christmas. What else would any respectful child do, right?

At the University of Colorado, my retreat from religion was influenced heavily by two factors: One, the humanistic philosophy that seeped into my thinking through nearly every class I attended, and two, the self-satisfying hedonistic lifestyle that dominated college life on and off campus. It seemed rational and liberating to move forward with God gone, or at least far away.

But then it happened. The Hound of Heaven began chasing me down in earnest. On the home front, my girlfriend Ann (now my wife of over fifty years) became a Christian and challenged me to join her in the journey. Then I made a friend in Oregon, where I was working in a lumber mill, who had just decided to become a follower of Jesus. Clive was on his way to Canada, hoping to avoid being drafted into the Vietnam War, when he decided to stop in Eugene to throw some pottery. We ended up living together for the summer and talking theology as we explored the mountains, beaches, and riverways of the Northwest. I could relate to Clive's brand of Christianity way more than what I grew up with.

And then there was the season I spent hitchhiking around Europe with Greg. In nearly every country we visited, God had planted someone we would bump into who would reinforce the notion that getting to know Jesus was the way to go. I've often wondered since then if God commissioned a handful of angels disguised as humans to pester us.

One gentleman in particular stands out. He greeted us one morning on the outskirts of the border town of Carlisle, England. We were hiking around the city and happened on a beautiful old stone church. This rather large, bearded man with a thick Scottish accent approached us with a staff in hand and introduced himself as Mr. Johnson.

"So, lads, ma' hunch is ya hail from across the Pond; some part of America, no doubt. Would you like to peek inside this wee kirk? It's not forbidden."

We spent an hour or more touring the property with Mr. Johnson, frequently resting on a bench or pew to listen to his stories about the church and the importance of its history. Woven into his monologues were questions he asked Greg and me about our spiritual inclinations. We were both rather vague in our responses.

So fascinating was this elderly Scot that we invited him to join us for dinner at our hostel to talk with him some more. We asked him to return for breakfast the following morning before our train left for London. In one way or another, he encouraged us to become acquainted with Jesus and draw near to him as we journeyed through Europe and life. Greg and I agreed as we departed Carlisle that we hoped we might grow as winsome and spiritually minded as Mr. Johnson by the time we reached his age. To this day, his words and manner have served as a compass to keep me on the path he prescribed.

When I returned from Europe, I set out in earnest to debunk or affirm the narrative these Bible-thumpers kept harassing me with. Nine months later, after many hours of poring over the Bible, asking questions, debating believers, and searching my soul, I crossed over to begin living the never-ending story: David in Wonderland, I call it. I realized that I had been trying to resolve a philosophical quandary rather than to know my heavenly Father personally. Now that I knew him by his Spirit in me, I saw each day with new eyes, a kind of double vision whereby a second lens allowed me to increasingly see all things as God sees them.

Ann and I were married on May 16, 1971. I had just turned twenty-one, and Ann was almost halfway through her twentieth year. Papa died in April the following year. Before he passed, he had invited me to join him in the real estate development business after I graduated. Dad had been concentrating on the family-owned lumber yard chain in four states, and Papa was focusing on residential and commercial real estate development. As we discussed the prospects of my coming to work in the family business, I explained my spiritual awakening and desire to return to campus as a campus minister after graduation. I had been offered a position with a ministry organization at the University of Colorado called Campus Ambassadors. Papa was disappointed but encouraged me to follow my heart. I had gained so much insight, meaning, joy, and purpose through my decision to follow Christ that I felt compelled to share God's Good News with other students.

Fast-forward: After finishing my college education at CU, I spent the next eight years in Christian ministry on the campuses of CU and the University of California in Santa Cruz while earning my master's degree in biblical theology from Denver Seminary. Ann and I enjoyed learning to be married and doing our best to raise three wonderful kids—Allison, Grant, and Lane—while we developed enduring relationships with many students and neighbors during these years.

I left campus ministry in 1981. Ann and I returned to our roots in Fort Collins, where we still reside. I went to work with my father, brother, and brother-in-law in the family business, which was predominantly focused on real estate development and homebuilding.

Ann and I have often expressed our gratitude for calling this community home. It would require volumes to tell you more. In general, though, I echo what my dad would regularly proclaim when speaking of Northern Colorado: "Good, good, good."

During my years growing up in Fort Collins and for some years after Ann and I were married, our family frequently traveled to Enid to visit my mom's parents, other family members, and some friends my parents grew up with in the town that held so much of my ancestors' history. People were forever telling me stories about my relatives: aunts, uncles, great grandparents, grand uncles, grand aunts, cousins twice removed on my mom's side, thrice removed on my dad's. Some of them I met personally, others I could hardly figure out where they belonged on the family tree. Having been born in Enid and regularly reminded of my cultural heritage, I sensed a soulful attachment to the town and its people in some unexplainable way.

There was in the back of my mind the lingering questions prompted by Papa's journals I'd discovered shortly after he died. I wondered if anyone in our family in Enid, or on the planet, knew of his two years with the young Keetoowah woman, Awinita, in Forest Canyon.

PART THREE:
Full Circle

43

Professor's Farewell

istance and time, marriage and children, allotted me little opportunity to visit Enid often. However, I was able to visit my birthplace on a memorable occasion, this time with my daughter, Allison. Especially meaningful was a tour of my mom's childhood home graciously granted to us by the then-current owners, Stephen and Wendy O'Neill, and their charming young daughter, Mary. My mother, who was rapidly failing physically, joined Alli and me on the tour via FaceTime from her home in Fort Collins. What a joy for her to see her house and be introduced to the amiable owners as we went from room to room with iPad in hand.

"It looks the same," Mom delightfully observed as we panned each part of the house with the camera. Mary accompanied Mom via FaceTime to her bedroom above the garage, which was my mother's bedroom growing up. Once there, Mary faced the camera and proudly declared, "This is where I come to use my imagination."

"Me too!" Mom enthusiastically replied.

Mom died the following year.

In the fall of 2003, Ann and I took a road trip to Enid to renew friendships with family and old acquaintances still living there. We saw many of the homes once occupied by my grandparents on both my mother's and father's side, as well as the original downtown locations of Long-Bell Lumber and my great-great-grandfather's livery stable. We even located what was believed to be the original homesite Jack and Elizabeth Everitt carved out of the side of a hill in 1893 near what is now Government Springs Park.

"How does seeing all of this make you feel?" Ann asked me.

"Honestly, it's pretty awesome to relive so much of my family's history in my head and imagine what Enid was like during the last hundred years. There are so many memories of my visits here growing up. It's quite overwhelming to see the house on Wynona Ave. where my mom was raised. I still have images of our family's Thanksgiving dinners in that stately old house and all of the good times visiting with Mom's parents, Meme and Dada, who remained there until a few years before they died."

During Ann's and my excursion to Enid on this occasion, we caught wind of a Native American celebration. The Southern Heights Annual Pow Wow Celebration was underway just south of downtown. I was unexpectedly reminded that the Indian woman Papa highlighted in his journals was born in Enid. I thought it would be interesting to see if some of the Indian traditions Papa mentioned would possibly be displayed at the Pow Wow.

I hadn't opened his journals since I found them in 1972, the year he died. Over the course of the thirty-plus years since I first read them, I had wondered if what they chronicled was true. It seemed an unbelievable story. Yet, why would he have hidden them and told no one about his time in Forest Canyon if it really didn't happen?

"What do you think?" I asked Ann. "Shall we check out the Pow Wow?"

"Sure. It will be fun and something different."

The outdoor events were crowded when we arrived. There was Pow Wow dancing and singing, as well as several interesting displays and educational opportunities to learn about the customs and beliefs of the first Native American settlements in this region of Oklahoma before it became a state.

After two hours of wandering around the grounds, I suggested we move on and drive somewhere for dinner. "I've seen enough, and it's getting hot."

Ann nodded her agreement.

On the way to our car, we walked by a makeshift outdoor pavilion where a large crowd, mostly Indians, had gathered to listen to an Indian woman giving a talk.

"David, let's sit and listen for a minute," Ann suggested. "It might be interesting." She quickly found us a spot on the grass near the back of the pavilion.

The speaker was well into her talk; we leaned in to hear what she was saying. She appeared on the verge of tears. Her voice quivered as she spoke. She paused, took a deep breath, and said, "I want to tell you how meaningful it is to be with you this afternoon. What an honor it is that you would celebrate my retirement as a part of your Pow Wow here in Enid."

Enthusiastic crowd members clapped, stomped, pounded drums, and blew flutes while chanting "*hey hey hey hey o'whah*" in appreciation of their *Ghigau* (Beloved Woman).

"It has been my delight to have taught at Tahlequah High School," the woman continued, "as well as at Fort Lewis College in Colorado, and Bacone College in Muskogee, totaling nearly forty years in the classroom. I have had the privilege of teaching many of you. In some instances, I have taught three generations of your families. Why, I was hardly older than some of you who were in my classes at Tahlequah during the 1950s. *Wado*. Thank you.

"But there is another reason I am blessed to be with you in Enid today. Perhaps some of you have wondered why my name is Enid. It is not a coincidence. Many of you knew my mother, Awinita, who lived among you for twelve years before she walked on. Most of you do not know that your town, Enid, is where she was born in 1902. But she did not grow up here. Before she was two years old, she and her parents, Laniyah and Slow Walker, were forced to leave Enid because of the violence that rose against them and threatened their lives. For over sixty-five years, Awinita lived in exile from Enid, confident that one day she would return to her tribe and settle again in her place of birth to complete her circle of life. She often reminded me of this hope, quoting Jesus's promise recorded by his beloved Apostle, John: 'Your love and trust in me will bring the Father's love to you—full circle' (John 16:27).

"No doubt Awinita spoke with some of you about her incredible life since leaving Enid as an infant. For those who do not know the story, I will not detain you with the details now. Suffice it to say that my mother spent nearly the first twenty years of her life isolated deep in the mountains of Colorado with her parents. After tragically losing both of them, she was discovered living alone in Forest Canyon by a young White man who stayed with her until they reluctantly parted ways. Mother told me of the love that grew between them, but that they both unhappily accepted that living together in Mother's forest cabin was not a reasonable option.

"After her young lover, whom she called Oginalii, left her in the canyon, my mother discovered she was pregnant. When I was born, Mother called me Enid because your town was not only her place of birth, but also where my father was born. She told me that although they would never meet again, their love for each other was marked by their common birthplace. She named me Enid to express this shared love."

The woman paused for a drink of water and to collect her emotions.

"Some have asked if I ever looked for my father, or if I am bitter toward him for abandoning Mother in Forest Canyon. Let me say this: First, my father never even knew I was born or that my mother was pregnant when he left Forest Canyon. One cannot abandon someone he has never met.

"Second, I am so grateful to have had a life to live. Without my father, I would never have walked this earth. Although there have been hardships along the way, to have been awake to Creator and all he has made, to have known my mother and so many others who have blessed me, to have discovered my purpose in life and how meaningful the whole experience has been would not have been my joy if not for my father, Oginalii. As Mother taught me as a child, 'God speaks to us in what happens to us.'"

As Enid made her closing remarks, my mind raced as I made the unbelievable connection between what she said about herself and what I had read in Papa's journals so many years before. I turned to Ann and could see in her eyes the same heightened emotions I felt.

"I've got to talk with her," I told Ann. "Let's ask her to join us for dinner."

Ann nodded. "This is going to be awkward."

After Enid finished speaking and the crowd broke up, I approached the stage and got in line to talk to her. I rehearsed what I would say: "Hi, my name is David, and your father is my grandfather!"

When it was my turn to speak with Enid, I was virtually tongue-tied. Still, somehow, I managed to introduce myself and mention that I knew her father and would like to explain something about him if she would join me and my wife, Ann, for dinner.

At first, she was skeptical. But with enough information to demonstrate that I was for real and with Ann at my side helping to set her at ease, Enid agreed to come downtown with us to Tia Juana's restaurant.

44

Reunion

After the three of us were seated, I explained to Enid how grateful we were for her taking a chance to join us. She was gracious and had no hesitation in engaging in casual conversation before our dinners were served. Then she got to the reason for being together.

"You have told me enough to make me believe you know of my father," Enid began. "How have you come by this knowledge, and what more can you tell me of him?"

I shared my family history and our long connection with Enid. I told her about finding my grandfather Les's hidden journals and reading his account of meeting and living with Enid's mother, Awinita, in Forest Canyon.

This revelation left Enid speechless and seemingly overcome with emotion.

"Are you suggesting that your grandfather, Les, is Oginalii, and that you and I are related?"

"Yes," I replied. "I know it's hard to believe, but I'm your half-nephew, and my father, Bob, is your half-brother. He's the son of the man you and your mother call Oginalii. We are your blood relatives."

Enid's lips trembled, then she quietly wept into her napkin.

After she composed herself, we exchanged a flood of questions and answers until long after we had finished eating. Still, there was so much more we all wanted to know. At one point, I suggested Enid come to Fort Collins to visit Ann and me. We could introduce her to my father and her other relatives on our side of the family.

"I would be delighted to let you read your father's journals and learn of his time with your mother in Forest Canyon," I told Enid. "If you like, it would be my greatest joy to take you into the mountains above Estes Park to where your life began. As for me, I'm curious about what you've learned from your mother about her relationship with my grandfather and where you and Awinita went after leaving Forest Canyon."

Enid said she would consider visiting us but needed time to process all she had just learned. "Let me sort all of this out in my mind," Enid finally said. "I am awestruck by this unexpected news and unsure how to respond. Can we talk in a few days?"

"Take all the time you need," I said.

I could tell she wondered if her life would take a new trajectory because of meeting members of her family whom she did not know existed until today. How would learning the unfinished story of her father affect her future?

"Thank you for reaching out to me," Enid said. "I am stunned, but at the same time excited. At long last, I can learn my father's fate after he left Forest Canyon. I know this: God speaks to us in what happens to us. He breathes meaning into everything. I am listening."

45

Return to Forest Canyon

nid did come to stay with Ann and me in Fort
Collins for some months in 2003. During her time
here, she was warmly greeted by the entire Everitt
family. She and my dad, her half-brother, Bob, spent a
considerable amount of time sharing stories. They had
so much to tell each other, and they bonded as kindred
spirits. Enid, now eighty years old, commented that,
at last, she had a complete family. Granted, both her
mother and father had walked on, but with the life she
had with Awinita as a child, and with the life of Oginalii
she learned of through her mother's memories, Papa's
journals, and now three generations of his descendants,
the circle had been completed. Her spirits were high.

"My joy is full," she regularly told her newly discovered family.

As Enid shared her story, our family learned that
literally days after Les walked out of Forest Canyon,
members of the Ute tribe came upon the pregnant
Awinita and insisted she winter with them. "Mother

gave birth to me on the fourteenth of April 1922, the year after she left Forest Canyon to live with the White River Utes near Grand Lake on the western slope of the Rocky Mountains."

My sister, Claudia, told Enid that April 14 was not only her birthday but also the same day Oginalii was born twenty-one years before. The discovery caught both Enid and Claudia off guard. After the coincidental fact sank in, they smiled at one another and laughed.

Enid then continued with her story. "I know, now that the Utes came in the wake of the West Wind to answer Oginalii's prayer that Awinita would be safe without him," Enid said. "And indeed, she was safe; not only safe but content. In time, Mother and I went to live with another tribe in Southern Colorado, where there were better opportunities for us than among the White River Utes."

"What did you and Awinita do in Southern Colorado?" Ann asked.

"Awinita secured an administrative position at Fort Lewis College in Durango," Enid replied. "It was the first college in the United States to offer education to Native Americans tuition-free. Everyone loved my mother, including Whites and Indians from several different tribes. She was very suited for her job and pleasant to everyone in her soft-spoken way.

"It was at Fort Lewis that I began my education in American Indian Studies. I learned of the tragic history of my people, and many other native tribes in the early years of our country, tragedies that are still unfolding to this day. My emerging career in American Indian Studies brought Mother and me to Oklahoma in 1945, where I taught in Tahlequah and at Bacone Indian University in Muskogee."

"That must have been very rewarding," Ann said.

Enid nodded, then shifted the conversation to Awinita. "Mother always wanted to return to her place of birth. She moved to Enid in 1970 to live with her fellow Keetoowah while I continued teaching at Bacone two hundred miles east. Eventually, I moved to Enid so I could care for Mother, whose health was failing. She died in 1982 at eighty, among her beloved people."

Unbeknownst to either family until Enid's visit to Fort Collins, Papa's wife, Memo, died the same year. We were dumbstruck to learn that the two loves of Les's life walked on together.

Enid went back to teaching at Bacone College until she retired in 2003. That was the year Ann and I discovered her at the Pow Wow, which was held to honor her distinguished career instructing Indians from the many tribes living in Oklahoma and the surrounding states.

One evening, while Enid was with us, I gave her a copy of the eulogy from her father's funeral. In it, Reverend Baird eloquently spoke of Les's commitment to Jesus Christ. After Enid finished reading the eulogy, she looked up and said in a trembling voice, "Mother told me once that she never knew if Oginalii would continue to worship Creator Set Free once he returned to his home. She would be so overjoyed to know how positively her many talks with Oginalii influenced his spiritual journey and the impact for good he had on so many during his life."

Enid teared up as she read the final words of the eulogy out loud: "If there is a theme to any life, it seems so clearly to me that the theme of Les Everitt's life might be: 'But his was a God-centered life.'"

It was during her stay in Fort Collins that Enid disclosed to us that she had recently been diagnosed with cancer.

"The doctors said my cancer is incurable and that it will eventually take my life. Although I have no pain, I do tire more quickly these days and have lost much of my strength."

Even so, when I offered to drive her up Trail Ridge Road from where she could look down into Forest Canyon, she readily agreed to go. At a wide spot on the road just after Rainbow Curve, I stopped and helped Enid out of the car. We slowly walked beyond the trailhead of the Ute Trail to a place overlooking the deep, narrow canyon where Awinita and Oginalii met and lived and where Enid was conceived. The impact of this place on all three of their lives was felt by both of us as we stared into the canyon.

Enid leaned into the wind atop the ridge, looking down through the thick forest at the silver stream at the bottom of the canyon. She lingered in silence for the longest time, then chanted a song in Keetoowah. When she finished, she said to me, "I desire to have my remains buried near my mother in Enid. But after I have walked on, will you come to this spot and throw some little remains of my ashes to the wind that the Great Spirit might take them to this valley where I was conceived? I would be so grateful."

And so it was that a few months after returning to her namesake in 2004, Enid walked on, and her ashes were buried next to her mother. Several of us from her Colorado family came to join with friends from her tribe and some of her Enid neighbors to honor this remarkable woman.

A small group of Keetoowah joined my family and me in Colorado some days after the burial ceremony in Oklahoma. We cast some of Enid's ashes into Forest Canyon from the spot where she and I had stood the year before.

After the small crowd dispersed, I stayed behind to say a prayer of thanks and to toss a small white stone and a silver dollar into the canyon to follow the ashes to the place where they belonged.

About the Author

D. Grant Everitt lives in Fort Collins, Colorado, with his lovely wife, Ann. Domiciled with them in their backyard ponds are frogs and fish, enjoyed by visiting predators and kids in the neighborhood. David is intrigued by lots of things and enjoys lots of fascinating people. He also likes to be with himself sometimes.